SIREN
Publishing

Ménage Everlasting

Liberation

SLICK ROCK 16

BECCA VAN

Liberation

After being shot in a bank hold-up, Delta Sykes packs her bags and heads to Slick Rock, Colorado. She is lucky enough to see a real estate advertisement for the sale of the town's diner and decides a change is a good way to find a semblance of peace.

However, she doesn't expect to meet and be attracted to three men—or to have them return the attraction. No one has ever looked at her twice or treated her like a normal human being, and she keeps waiting for the other shoe to drop.

Major, Rocco, and Ace Porter know Delta is the woman they've been waiting for. However, trying to convince the hearing-impaired Delta they aren't stringing her along is harder than they thought.

When Delta ends up in danger, the men rally around her to protect her and she finally concedes to try a relationship with them.

Just when they think the danger has passed, Delta is snatched right out from under their noses.

Genre: Contemporary, Ménage a Trois/Quatre, Western/Cowboys
Length: 65,105 words

LIBERATION

Slick Rock 16

Becca Van

Siren Publishing, Inc.
www.SirenPublishing.com

A SIREN PUBLISHING BOOK

LIBERATION
Copyright © 2017 by Becca Van

ISBN: 978-1-64010-953-7

First Publication: December 2017

Cover design by Les Byerley
All art and logo copyright © 2017 by Siren Publishing, Inc.

PUBLISHER
Siren Publishing, Inc.
www.SirenPublishing.com

DEDICATION

This book is dedicated to all my readers. Although I haven't been around much due to a long illness, you are all in my heart. If it wasn't for you all, I don't know if I'd still be writing or even still here. So thank you from the bottom of my heart.

Love always,
Becca xxoo

ABOUT THE AUTHOR

My name is Becca Van. I live in Australia with my wonderful hubby of many years, as well as my two children.

I read my first romance, which I found in the school library, at the age of thirteen and haven't stopped reading them since. It is so wonderful to know that love is still alive and strong when there seems to be so much conflict in the world.

I dreamed of writing my own book one day but, unfortunately, didn't follow my dream for many years. But once I started I knew writing was what I wanted to continue doing.

I love to escape from the world and curl up with a good romance, to see how the characters unfold and conflict is dealt with. I have read many books and love all facets of the romance genre, from historical to erotic romance. I am a sucker for a happy ending.

For all titles by Becca Van, please visit
www.bookstrand.com/becca-van

LIBERATION

Slick Rock 16

BECCA VAN
Copyright © 2017

Prologue

Delta Sykes smiled as she followed Mr. Curtis with her gaze. He came in each week and she looked forward to his visits. He was such a nice man and he took the time to speak to her about everyday life rather than just getting on with business like all the other customers did. She shifted her gaze to her next customer, the smile sliding from her lips when she met cold gray eyes, and then she began to shake. Her heart slammed against her sternum, her breath hitched in her throat and then she began to pant. Sweat broke out all over her body and her knees felt as if they were about to buckle, but she locked them in place.

Fear as she'd never known before coursed through her veins with the flight-or-fight hormones, but there was nowhere to run. The New City Bank in Chicago was full of customers and staff. Plus, she was stuck in her locked teller cubicle with no way out unless she used the key to unlock the door.

Delta stared down the barrel of the gun, but when her brain finally kicked in she noticed that the gun wasn't what a normal firearm looked like. This one was white and looked as if it was made of plastic. She decided then and there that although this asshole was trying to rob the bank, she wasn't about to hand over any cash to him. He couldn't shoot anyone with a fake gun, so hopefully no one would get hurt.

She glanced quickly toward the security guard and cursed mentally when she saw he was talking and laughing with a gorgeous young woman who'd just entered the bank. No help would be coming from him. All Cory ever seemed to do was flirt with women when he should have been alert and watching all the customers so that nothing untoward would happen. It was a little too late for that.

Even though Delta couldn't hear the man talking since she was completely deaf, she could read his lips. "Give me all your money."

She frowned and shook her head as she surreptitiously lifted her hand toward the button which would set off the silent alarm.

"Don't move, bitch, or I'll shoot you."

Delta's heart was pounding so hard it almost hurt, but she wasn't about to let this bastard intimidate her. She moved the inch and just before she hit the silent alarm button, he lifted the fake white gun up higher and he pulled the trigger.

Shock had her blinking when something slammed into her shoulder and as she looked down and saw blood was already soaking into her white blouse, agony ripped into her shoulder, up her neck and down her arm. Delta opened her mouth and screamed. She had no idea if she was screaming loudly or whether her voice was only a husky, rasping sound, since she couldn't hear herself, but since her throat hurt she guessed she was screaming at the top of her lungs.

Everything from then on seemed to happen in slow motion. The robber turned away from her, and for a few seconds she thought he was going to start shooting all the innocent people. That was until she saw him falling onto the floor. Blood pooled rapidly underneath his body, and when she glanced toward the entrance, she was relieved to see that Cory had his weapon in his hand and there was smoke coming out of the end of the barrel.

Delta swayed on her feet when she got dizzy. When her knees gave out she grabbed for the edge of the counter, but missed. She cried out in agony when she hit the floor, her injured shoulder connecting first, and even though she tried to keep the encroaching darkness at bay, she couldn't. With a sigh, she gave into the black abyss with relief.

Chapter One

Major sat back after eating his dinner with a replete sigh. He'd heard there was a new chef working at the diner, and after the wonderful reviews the food had gotten, he and his brothers had decided to find out for themselves.

He'd ordered steak and vegetables, and the meat had been so tender it almost melted in his mouth. "That was fucking delicious."

"My chicken was the best damn roast chicken I've ever tasted." Rocco, one of Major's brothers licked his lips and patted his flat belly. "How was your lasagna, Ace?"

"If I wasn't so stuffed I would have ordered another one," Ace, Major's youngest brother, answered with a smile.

"Has anyone seen this new wonder chef?" Rocco asked as he glanced toward the diner counter.

"Not that I've heard," Rocco replied.

Major was too curious to let this go. He raised his finger to call one of the waitresses over.

"What can I get you?" the teenage girl asked with a blush.

Major glanced at her name badge before meeting her gaze again. "Cindy, could you get the chef out here please?"

"Is there a problem?" Cindy asked as she eyed the empty dinner plates.

"No, honey, we just wanted to give our compliments to the chef. That was the best damn steak I've ever tasted, and my brothers said their food was delicious, too."

Cindy smiled. "I will pass on your compliments but I'm sorry to say, the chef doesn't like coming out front."

Major frowned and crossed his arms over his chest. Was the chef so far up himself he didn't like interacting with his customers? If so, the asshole wouldn't last long in this small Colorado town.

"Why the hell not?"

Major scowled at his impetuous brother. Ace was always rushing in without thinking.

Cindy's blush deepened and she shifted on her feet. "The chef is very shy."

That may have been true, but it wasn't the whole truth. Major didn't need to be a genius to figure out that the waitress was hedging since she'd glanced toward the left. She met his gaze again. "Did you want to order something else?"

Rocco cleared his throat. "I'll have the apple pie with ice-cream, please."

"I have the chocolate self-saucing pudding and ice-cream," Ace gave his order.

"I don't want any dessert, but we all would like another round of coffee."

"Sure. I'll be back to refill your mugs after I place your order." Cindy scurried away.

Major wished he and his brothers hadn't chosen a booth in the back of the diner. He wanted to see whoever took the order from the waitress through the serving window, but he was too far away. His curiosity wouldn't let up, and without conscious thought he stood and moved down the aisle between the tables and booths. He was just in time to see a small hand take the order slip from Cindy before disappearing. No other part of the person's body showed in the window.

He hurried back to the booth and sat.

"Well?" Ace smirked at him.

"Didn't see anything except for a small hand."

"You think the new chef is a woman?" Rocco asked.

Major shrugged. "How the hell am I supposed to know that? That hand could have belonged to one of the kitchen hands."

"Someone has to know who the new chef is?"

Major nodded and then glanced toward the door when the bell above tinkled. His smile returned when he saw his friends, Ridge, Bull, and Rocky enter with their wife, Carly. He'd met Carly years ago when he and his brothers had visited his father's brother's ranch. It was good to see his three friends and their woman so happy and in love.

"Hi guys," Carly greeted with a smile.

Major rose, took Carly's hand in his and tugged her into his arms. "How are you doing, sweetheart?"

"Good." Carly hugged him back before drawing away. "How are you all doing? Have you finished with all the new fences? I know the barn and sheds are all finished."

"It would be hard to miss since our ranch butts up against yours." Major smiled. "You're full of energy. You haven't been eating too much chocolate, have you?"

"A girl can never eat too much chocolate." Carly giggled. "We wanted to check out the new chef. Since the diner was sold there hasn't been an empty seat in the place."

Ridge hooked an arm around Carly's waist and guided her toward the booth opposite theirs. Bull and Rocky sat on the other side of the table.

"We've finished putting up the new fences," Rocco answered one of Carly's questions.

Ace leaned forward so he could see Carly around Rocco. "Do you know who bought the diner?"

Carly shook her head. "Rumors have been rife, but that's to be expected in a small rural farming town. Although more and more people seem to be moving to Slick Rock." She sighed and her eyes glazed over for a moment. Bull must have seen the sadness in his wife's eyes, too, because he reached across the table and clasped her hand in his.

Major glanced out through the large window and into the waning light. Carly was right. More and more people were moving away from busy stressful city lives looking for a slower more relaxed pace of life. There was a new housing estate on the west side of town and he'd heard the sheriffs, Luke Sun-walker and Damon Osborn, talking about hiring on more men. He just hoped that the town didn't get too big too quickly.

He and his brothers had moved to Slick Rock two years ago. It hadn't been a hard decision since their parents had died when they were still little kids. He, Rocco, and Ace had been brought up by their grandparents and had often stayed the summer with their friends to give their grandparents a break by taking care of three boisterous boys. Luckily, they'd lived close to the Frost men. The friendship they'd forged way back when had survived and would continue to survive for years. The six of them were more like brothers than best friends.

As soon as they'd finished high school, they'd headed straight into the military, one after the other. There was just over a year's difference between him and Rocco, and only ten months between Rocco and Ace. They'd been inseparable as kids and still were. They'd all ended up in the SEALs and had even done a couple of stints in Delta Force.

The last mission had gone fubar. Major, Rocco, and Ace had been lucky to escape without injury. A couple of their teammates hadn't been as lucky, but at least none of them had lost their lives. When they hit the States he and his brothers had all decided enough was enough and retired.

They'd headed to Slick Rock to attend his friends' and Carly's wedding. Major and his brothers had been astounded by the number of polyandrous relationships in and around the small regional town.

He'd taken note of the way the citizens of Slick Rock had treated the people in those unusual relationships and he'd been pleasantly surprised that they'd been accepting. He, Rocco, and Ace had shared a few women between them from time to time while on leave, and though those women had known upfront that they weren't looking for anything serious, Major had loved every second of the experience. His excitement and desire had seemed more intense, and the women had left with big smiles on their faces.

After seeing how happy Carly and the other women in town were, he and his brothers had decided they wanted to share a woman, too. It had been just over two years since they'd bought the ranch next to Ridge's, Bull's and Rocky's, but they hadn't met a woman who was right for them.

It wasn't that they didn't have any choices since single women seemed to throw themselves at him and his brothers. They could have had women in their beds on a regular basis, but fucking for the sake of slaking his lust was real old. Major wanted to go home to the same woman each and every night. He wanted to build a solid, loving relationship that would weather the storms that tested their mettle. He wanted to have kids and have a member of the opposite sex love him in return. Not because he had a tall, fit body and a passably good looking face. Not because he was a notch on the belt of a woman hell-bent on getting laid by a retired soldier or a cowboy.

Major wanted to hold the same woman in his arms night after night. He and his brothers had been celibate since relocating to Slick Rock, but thankfully they'd all been too busy setting up their ranching operation to even think about getting their rocks off.

The first twelve months they'd all practically fallen into bed and had been asleep as soon as their heads had hit the pillow. The house had been rundown and small. They'd gutted the insides and extended. After the house had been finished, they'd begun working on the outside. The barn had been dangerous with its sagging roof and rotting beams and trusses. However, now that everything was done except for working the land and keeping the animals safe and fed, they had more time on their hands. They were no longer spending sixteen to eighteen hours running from one chore to another.

Nighttime was the worst. The loneliness seemed to encroach in the darkest hours, and the yearning to meet that one special women who would fit perfectly between him and his brothers had become an incessant craving. Sometimes Major wondered if they'd ever meet the right woman. Maybe he was going to have to accept that working their new ranch was it.

"What are you thinking so deeply about?" Rocco nudged his foot under the table.

"Nothing much," Major murmured, and while he tried to stop his gaze from wondering over to their friends and Carly, he couldn't seem to help himself.

Rocco knew him too well. "You're pining."

Major glared at his brother before turning his eyes toward the window. The sun had gone down half an hour ago, and while it wasn't late, it wasn't early either. Sunrise came way too early.

"Where the hell is our dessert?" Ace scowled toward the diner's counter.

"Give the girl a chance, little brother," Major said. "This place is packed and she's the only waitress working."

"The new owner better get his finger out of his ass and hire on some more people. If the customers have to wait too long for their orders, they'll stop coming."

"Let me out." Carly nudged Ridge's arm.

"What's wrong?" Ridge asked as he stood.

Carly scooted to the edge of the seat before standing. "Nothing's wrong."

Major watched Carly as she hurried toward the waitress and spoke quietly to her. The girl looked relieved when she began nodding. She pointed toward something on the other side of the counter.

Carly patted Cindy on the arm, skirted the counter, grabbed an apron, wrapped it around her waist and went to the serving window. She picked up the plates of food under the warming light and took them to a table.

"Shit!" Ridge took a step toward his wife, but Bull grabbed his arm and shook his head.

"If you want to sleep in our wife's bed tonight, I'd sit my ass back down."

"She shouldn't be—" Ridge cut himself off and rubbed the back of his neck.

"Our wife is generous and has a huge heart," Rocky said. "Are you going to stop her from helping out that girl when you can see she needs help?"

"Fuck." Ridge sat back in his seat, crossed his arms over his chest and stared at Carly.

Major bit the inside of his cheek but he couldn't stop the smile forming when Ace snickered. Rocco chuckled and tried to cover the sound up by coughing. It didn't work. Ridge scowled at them before gazing at his wife again.

Fifteen minutes later, Cindy filled all their coffee mugs and headed toward the serving window. She turned and headed in their direction before placing the desserts in front of Ace and Rocco.

"Sorry for the wait."

"No worries, honey. Did the other waitresses call in sick?" Major asked.

Cindy glanced away, shook her head and rushed back toward the serving window.

"What the hell is going on?" Rocco frowned. "The last owner had no trouble hiring staff. The owner must be a real asshole."

"You're jumping to conclusions," Bull said. "Most of the waitstaff were college students. They might have all graduated and moved away."

"What about the high school kids?" Ace asked. "Surely some of them want to earn some spending money? Something weird is going on here."

Major was in agreement about the weird part. He glanced toward Carly as he took a sip of his coffee. He moaned as the delicious flavor burst on his taste buds. When he saw Carly nodding and gesturing with her hands, he frowned.

"What the hell is your wife doing?"

Since Ridge was already facing the right way and saw everything Carly did, he just shrugged. Bull and Rocky turned to glance at her over their shoulders.

"She looks like she's trying to mime or something."

"Why would she—"

Bull interrupted Ace's question. "I've seen something like that before."

"Where? When?" Rocco asked.

"A buddy of ours ended up with hearing damaging after serving. He couldn't hear worth a damn for months and the only way he could communicate was with pen and paper or mime." Bull turned back around.

"You think the chef's deaf?" Ace asked.

"The chef or the kitchen hand Carly's trying to communicate with."

"We'll find out when she's finished with her good deed." Rocky sipped at his coffee.

It was another half hour before Carly came back to her husbands. She sat down with a sigh and snuggled into Ridge when he slung an arm around her shoulders.

"Why aren't there more waitresses working here?" Ridge asked.

Carly sat up straight and crossed her arms under her breasts. The scowl on her face, the firm set of her uplifted chin, and the fire in her eyes told of her anger.

"The new owner is also the chef. The poor woman is deaf and can't interview for new staff. She has an ad in the window but rumors have spread that she can't hear and no one other than Cindy has applied for work. Cindy is also proficient in sign language since her baby sister is deaf."

"That fucking stinks of prejudice," Rocky said angrily.

"Tell me about it." Carly gnawed on her lip. "We have to do something to help, but I don't know what."

"I have an idea," Major said.

"What?" Carly met his gaze.

"Why don't you and some of the other women do the interviewing for the owner?"

Carly slapped her hand against her forehead. "Why didn't I think of that? I've been such an airhead lately."

"Don't stress about it, baby," Bull said. "It's just hormones."

"If I'm like this now, what am I going to be like in six months' time?"

"You're pregnant?" Ace asked.

Carly nodded.

Major resisted the urge to rub at his aching chest. For a few moments, he had no idea why he was feeling pain, but when he looked a little deeper, he realized he was jealous. Jealous that his friends had what he'd been pining for the last three or so years. However, he was also happy for them.

Rocco and Ace were already on their feet, slapping the guys on their backs before tugging Carly to her feet and hugging her. Major waited until his brothers had moved aside. He cupped Carly's face in his hands and smiled down at the pretty, young woman. "I'm so damn happy for you all. Congratulations, sweetheart."

"Thanks," Carly said, and then blinked when tears welled in her eyes.

Major dropped his hands from her face to her shoulders and then pulled her into him. He sighed when she wrapped her arms around his waist and hugged him back. Having Carly in his arms made the yearning to have his own special woman even more intense. With another sigh, this one of reluctance—not because he was attracted to her or had feelings for her, but because he was pining for the one woman that would complete him and his brothers—he stepped back. He offered his hand to shake with Ridge, Bull, and Rocky, and from the smiles on their faces, they were all very happy and excited that their woman was pregnant. As well they should be.

Carly cleared her throat, garnering everyone's attention. "Do you think the other women will help me help the diner's chef?"

Chapter Two

Damn! Fuck! Shit! What the hell am I doing? Delta mentally asked after cursing up a storm. She didn't normally swear in her head but she deigned it an appropriate time to do so.

Sometimes Delta wanted to give up and give into the tears that continued to threaten her outwardly composed façade.

She'd been advertising for waitstaff for the last three months and had even prepared written questions for the interviewees, but as soon as the young women realized that Delta was deaf, they'd left. She'd been metaphorically dumped on her ass so many times over the last six months, but she kept picking herself back up. Now she was so busy she barely had time to scratch herself, and she felt dreadful that Cindy was the only person in the diner that was responsible for taking orders, delivering food, clearing dishes, and wiping down tables. The poor teenager looked as harried as Delta felt.

The moment Delta got up at four in the morning she didn't stop running. She was exhausted, but she didn't have time to slow down let alone stop.

When she'd arrived in Slick Rock four months ago, she'd been giddy with excitement when she'd seen the for-sale sign in the diner window. After being shot at the bank she hadn't been able to stay. It had taken her over two months to recover physically with physiotherapy, but the moment she'd stepped back into the bank on her first day after being off so long with paid sick leave, Delta had lost it. She didn't even remember crouching on the floor with her arms over her head as if trying to protect herself. Nor did she remember passing out. What she did remember was the terrible tight pain that had clutched at her chest, at her heart, or the lack of oxygen. Apparently, she'd been panting so quickly and noisily she'd sounded like a bellows working at a forge.

The manager had called an ambulance and when she'd woken up in the hospital, again, a signing psychologist had been sitting at her bedside. She'd talked with Delta for hours listening to her remembering all the horrors of being held up at gunpoint—no matter that, at first, she'd thought the gun was a toy—and the pain and terror she'd experienced when she'd been shot.

She'd come to the conclusion that she couldn't work for a bank ever again. The psychologist had been wonderful, helping her to work out what she wanted to do next, and when Delta had revealed that she was a chef by trade and that her passion was actually cooking, she'd encouraged her to follow her dreams. She'd come across an old advert on the internet about the diner in Slick Rock, and even though she hadn't known if the place was still for sale, she'd packed her sparse belongings, found someone else to sublease the small one bedroom apartment, packed her car, and the rest was history.

When she'd seen the for-sale sign was up in the diner's window, looking a little faded from the spring and summer sun, she'd wanted to dance a jig. Instead, she'd entered the eatery, took a seat, and after ordering a coffee, started writing on her ever-present notepad. The owner had been an elderly woman who wanted to move to another state to live close to her pregnant daughter. It had been a win-win for both of them. At least that's what Delta had thought at the time. Now she wasn't so sure she'd made the right decision.

How the hell am I supposed to keep the doors open when I can't get anyone to hire on? What am I supposed to do? Why do some people think that just because I can't hear, that I'm physically disabled or don't have a brain?

Delta blinked when she saw a strange young woman come up to the serving window with an apron wrapped around her waist. She glanced at the order and table number, picked up the four plates, one balanced on each of her forearms, and then grasped the other two in her hands before she turned and started carrying the order away. She drew in a ragged breath of gratitude, glad that the stove and oven was off to the side of the window and no one could see her. She didn't like being the center of attention, especially when it already seemed she was the local town spectacle, since she was the new diner's owner as well as the chef. Add into the fact that she was deaf, which was no doubt spreading around town as well, she was more than happy to keep out of the spotlight.

When she'd first started working at the bank everyone had constantly stared at her as if she were an animal in a zoo exhibit, or a bug under a microscope. It had been very disconcerting and she felt very self-conscious and uncomfortable, but thankfully the novelty had worn off after a few months. Nonetheless, Delta had always felt as if she was on the outside looking in, and she'd often wondered if the manager had done that to her on purpose since she wasn't *normal* like the rest of the staff. She'd had to man a teller window off to the side of the room, separate from everyone else. It made her wonder if she had been targeted by that bastard who'd shot her because she'd been so secluded. A shiver of fear shot up her spine and she began to pant.

Delta quickly pushed those disconcerting, terrifying thoughts aside and got her mind back on the food she was cooking. She almost smiled when she realized that nearly all the men who entered her diner mostly ordered steak, but considering she was now living in a cattle ranching area, she wasn't surprised.

Since she wasn't in a big city that catered to a more sophisticated palette, Delta had decided to provide good hearty meals on her menu. Of course, there was the prerequisite cuts of steak, as well as lasagna, chicken dishes as well as salads, vegetables and pasta, which all seemed to go over well with the locals. She offered simple delicious down home cooking with a few added flares. The steak was always marinated with her own special blend of sauces, herbs and spices. Baking the pies was time consuming, and was why she was always up so early in the morning. She'd wanted to fill the glass domed containers she'd found in the kitchen with muffins and cakes, but there was just never enough time. If her day consisted of forty-eight hours instead of the twenty-four, she still wouldn't have enough time. Delta was lucky to get four hours sleep a night, and it was starting to show. Not that she cared since no one but Cindy ever saw her, and she wasn't about to wear make-up or concealer to try and hide the dark smudges under her eyes since she was hovering over a hot stove and oven all day long.

Delta had wanted to open her diner from five in the morning until midnight for any late comers or travelers, but she couldn't see that happening anytime soon. She opened her doors at eight and closed them at eight, and still only managed around four hours of shuteye. There was always food preparation for the next day to do, not to mention the cleaning. If she'd had the money to do so, she would have hired someone to come in and clean the kitchen as well as the tables, floors and restrooms, but she didn't.

The lump sum of money she'd received from the bank for being hurt at work had been enough to cover the cost of purchasing the diner, with a little left over to buy supplies. Until she had more staff and a better cash flow, everything fell to her.

Cindy came to the serving window, smiled at her for the first time that day, grabbed the next order under the warming lights and rushed away.

Delta finished plating the chicken and steak meals, and had just set them under the warmer when the other woman wearing one of the diner aprons stepped up to the opening. She shifted her gaze to the woman's mouth when she started to speak, but wasn't fast enough to catch the first bit of her sentence. She sighed inwardly, pointed to her ears and shook her head.

The woman caught on quickly, smiled, and nodded. "I'm Carly. Why don't you have more waitstaff?"

Delta hoped she didn't look as frustrated and depressed as she felt, but tried to explain using hand gestures. Carly looked puzzled but then turned to face Cindy when the teenager came up next to her. She could see Cindy's lips moving quickly as she explained her situation. When Carly turned to meet her gaze again, Delta took an instinctive step back.

Carly looked downright pissed. "Are you shitting me?"

Delta shook her head.

"I can't believe how fucking stupid people are."

Relief washed away Delta's wariness when she realized that Carly was angry on her behalf. She shrugged since there wasn't much else she could do.

Carly reached over and clasped Delta's wrist. "Will you let me help you? Please?"

She nodded enthusiastically. There was no way she was going to turn down help when it could mean the difference between making a go of things or folding. She'd been peeking on the customers every now and then, and knew that some of them were beginning to get irate at having to wait so long for their orders, and she didn't blame them one little bit. She gave the other woman a grateful smile. Carly nodded and turned back toward the dining section.

If Carly knew some people that needed work and they were willing to work for a deaf boss, she wasn't about to refuse. She'd already set out a list of staff with experience in certain areas she'd wanted to hire, but since she couldn't "speak" with anybody, it had been impossible. Now, maybe she would get the workers she needed and she would be able to concentrate on the food rather than everything else as well.

Her long-term goals were to have the diner open twenty-four-seven. The highway wasn't that far out of town. She was hoping to have signage placed on the edge of the highway to advertise her diner. There was always traffic on the roads with truck driver's and such. Maybe she could even get tourist buses to stop in for meals. Alas, that was a ways off yet. First, she had to get some staff to help her deal with the locals before trying to attract more clientele.

By the time Cindy left, Delta was dead on her feet. She was so tired she could barely keep her eyes open. She'd already cleaned the kitchen, and most of the dishes were washed and put away. Cindy had stacked the industrial-size dishwashers with all the plates, glasses, mugs, and utensils twice. While the first load had been washing, the efficient, trustworthy girl had wiped down all the tables and put any of the freestanding chairs up ready for the floor to be washed. There were a few pots and pans sitting on the counter near the sink that needed to be scrubbed, but she decided to mop the floor first.

She was halfway through the cleaning the floor when she caught movement from the corner of her eye. Delta turned her gaze toward the window and shivered as fear skittered up her spine, causing her chest to tighten and her lungs to expand and contract rapidly.

Three very tall, very muscular men were standing outside on the sidewalk leaning against a large truck. They seemed to be talking, but they weren't looking at each other. No, they were all watching her with avid intentness.

Delta's first instincts were to turn and run, but she couldn't seem to make her feet move. It felt as if they were glued to the floor. She had no idea how long she stood there frozen looking like an idiot, but when one of the men pushed up from the hood of the truck, the movement seemed to break her from her trance and she continued to mop the floor. It was really difficult to ignore them, but she did so as much as she could. When she was done, she bent to pick up the bucket of dirty soapy water and took a step toward the kitchen.

She didn't know if she'd stepped in a puddle of water or if she'd skidded because the floor was slick, but her feet went flying out from under her. She thought she might have cried out but really didn't have any idea. Her ass hit the floor first and then she was flat on her back. She'd lost her grip on the bucket and now she was drenched from head to feet.

Delta spluttered and mentally cursed as she tried to regain her breath. The fear which had coursed through her blood when she'd seen the three men was gone. Now all she felt was total humiliation. Her day had just gone from bad to worse. The scarred tissue around her shoulder began to throb and she wondered if she'd jolted the not-so-old-wound, but that was the least of her worries. Right now, she needed to get up off her ass, re-mop the floor, and then clean the pots and pans. And that was before she needed to start on tomorrow's food preparation. All she wanted to do was go and have a shower, crawl into bed and sleep a solid eight hours, but it wasn't to be.

She pushed herself upright and winced when her shoulder protested, and then she was gaping in shock. The three men who'd been outside were no longer outside. They'd somehow managed to unlock the door and they were hurrying toward her.

Ignoring the pain in her shoulder, she pushed backward using her hands and shoe-clad feet on the floor. It was easy to move when she was sitting in a big puddle of water. The man closest to her stopped walking toward her. Delta looked up. And up, and up, and up some more. The man was freaking huge. Even though she was sitting on her ass on the floor, she could tell he was way over six feet tall, probably closer to six-five or over. She couldn't help but notice his long, denim-encased legs, his thick, muscular thighs, or the bulge at his crotch as her gaze lifted. He had a flat belly, and while his cotton T-shirt wasn't tight, the material was clinging to him and she could see his abdomen was ripped. His pectoral muscles were bulging with strength and his biceps were huge. Even his neck had muscles. However, it was his face that had her heart arresting in her chest. He wasn't handsome in that classical-movie, pretty-boy way. He was handsome with a rugged strength and masculinity. There was also an aura of power and confidence that had the breath exploding from her lungs.

Delta closed her eyes when she realized she was staring like an enamored ninny, and after taking a few deep breaths and releasing them, she met his amazing gray-blue eyes. When he waved a hand in front of her face and pointed at his lips, she realized he knew she couldn't hear him. She stared at his mouth as he formed words. "Are you okay?" And to her exuberant surprise he signed the words as well.

Delta nodded.

He held his hand out toward her after signing. "Let me help you up."

She stared at his big manly hand and debated on whether she should accept the offer, but realized if she didn't, she would seem rude. She'd never been, and never would be, rude to another human being because she knew what it was like to be shunned and disparaged just because she was a little different. Taking another deep, fortifying breath, she put her small hand in his. The moment their hands touched skin to skin, her body lit up like the Fourth of July. A shiver worked up her spine as tingling heat traveled from her hand, up her arm, into her chest, and down toward her sex.

She gasped when her pussy seemed to swell and moisten, but she bit the inside of her cheek hoping to quell the shudder working through her body as he helped her to her feet. She couldn't help but wince when pain surged into her shoulder.

He cupped her face with his free hand, tilting her gaze up toward his face. "Where are you hurting, honey?"

For the first time in her life, Delta wished she could hear. It didn't matter that he was signing as well, and while she was grateful to find someone who could speak to her other than Cindy, she wished she hadn't contracted meningitis as a toddler. Because more than anything right now, she wanted to hear his voice. It took a second or two to get her brain to kick in so she could answer his question. There was no way she could speak the words, so she just shook her head again, hoping he'd understand she hadn't hurt herself when she'd slipped. She was shaking a little too much to sign, to speak back to him just yet. Other than a bruised ass, that was, and she wasn't about to tell him, so she shook her head. He was so damn tall, she felt downright small and petite, and she wasn't short, since she stood five foot six in height. The guy had a good foot or more on her.

Her breath hitched in her throat when he clasped her chin between his finger and thumb, bringing her gaze back up to his. She quickly lowered her eyes when she saw his lips move, following his talking hands from her periphery.

"I'm Major Porter and these are my brothers, Rocco and Ace." He pointed to each man as he said their name.

Delta couldn't believe how big, brawny and handsome they all were. She figured their parents must have had great genes to turn out three such good-looking men.

Rocco was an inch or so shorter than Major, and his hair was a shade or two darker than his brother's sandy brown hair, but he was just as well-built. His eyes were an amazing gray-green combination, and if she wouldn't have looked like an idiot she could have stared into those colorful orbs forever. Rocco's face was clean shaven, but Major had a light gruff along his jaw and chin, and yet both of them were sexy as hell.

She glanced toward Ace when he shifted on his feet and sucked in a deep breath. His eyes were pure gray and his hair was a chocolate brown hue. He was about an inch shorter than Major and an inch taller than Rocco, but he was also burly in the muscle department. All three men seemed to exude confidence and authority as well as a carnal sexuality that made her breathless.

When she realized she was once more standing there frozen in place while she checked the men over, her cheeks began to heat with embarrassment. She hoped she didn't look like an idiot school girl with her first crush, even if that's exactly what she felt like.

She brought her gaze back to Major's when he caressed her chin with his thumb.

"What's your name, honey?"

The heat in her cheeks intensified with guilt since she hadn't bothered to identify herself, but also because she couldn't answer him verbally. She'd had speech therapy lessons and knew how to shape words and even speak, but because she didn't know how loudly or softly she spoke, or what she sounded like, Delta had decided to keep her mouth shut. She stepped back from Major and turned toward the counter. She kept a stack of pens, pencils and pads on a shelf underneath and needed to get one so she could reply to his question. She'd glanced at the other two men and realized from their puzzled looks that they couldn't speak or understand sign language. It was rude to continue her conversation with Major leaving his brothers on the outside edge, because she knew all too well how that felt, since she'd been there her whole life.

When she walked across the still slick wet floor she was careful about where and how she placed her feet, but she been so intent on not falling on her ass again, she ended up bumping into a hard, warm brick wall.

She gasped when strong hands gripped her shoulder to steady her, and she cringed with pain as that gentle grip exacerbated her aching shoulder. She glanced up into Rocco's gray-green eyes and mouthed, "Sorry."

He was frowning down at her, and while all these men were strangers to her, she didn't feel as if she was in danger like she had earlier, and that was an anomaly to her. Ever since she'd been shot in the bank hold-up she'd been scared of the opposite sex. So why wasn't she scared now?

Before she could answer her own question, she was swept off her feet and up into Rocco's arms. She sucked in a surprised breath and had to swallow down a moan building in her chest. He smelled so good. The fragrance emanating from his skin was a mix of pine and citrus and it was so yummy she had the urge to lean up and lick his neck. She bit her lip instead.

Delta wasn't sure what he was doing and was as tense as a bowstring since she wasn't used to being picked up and manhandled. But when he set her on a chair one of the other men must have removed from on top of the tables and put her in it, she relaxed again. That was until he squatted down in front of her and placed his hands on her bare knees. A fission of heat caused goosebumps to form on her skin and race up all over her body.

She met his gaze and quickly glanced away again when she noticed he was watching her intently. He cupped one of her cheeks and brought her gaze back to his. Having his large, warm, manly hand against her skin felt so good, she had the urge to turn her head and kiss it or nuzzle into it. Nonetheless, she refrained.

"Did you hurt your shoulder?" Rocco asked.

She was about to shake her head no, but gazed over at Ace when he handed her a pen and paper. She'd been so intent on his brother, she hadn't even realized he'd moved away.

Delta nodded her thanks to Ace and took the pad and pen. She rested the paper on her lap and started to write. *My name is Delta Sykes. I just jarred an old injury, so, no, I'm not hurt.*

The breath in her lungs exploded in a gust when Ace and Major squatted in front of her on each side of Rocco. She inhaled deeply and tried to hold it, but she couldn't.

She felt hemmed in and her mind whirred back to the day of the bank hold-up. Sweat broke out over her skin and while she panted rapidly, she could barely breath. The intermittent tightness returned to her chest and dizziness assailed her. She wanted to get up and run, but her legs were trembling and felt as if they were the consistency of Jell-O.

Blackness encroached on the edge of her vision, and while she tried to get her roiling emotions back under control, there was no stopping them. She felt as if she was on a runaway train without any brakes and the end of the line was in sight. Delta didn't even notice she was swaying in her seat until Major and Rocco each clasped her upper arms. Just as she thought she was going to pass out, one of the men gently clasped the back of her neck and pushed her head down toward her knees.

Delta how no idea how long she stayed bent over but it felt as if a long time had passed. She was so ashamed and embarrassed of her reaction she didn't want to sit up straight and see the pity, or worse, callousness in their eyes, but she knew she couldn't hide out forever. So, after taking a deep, fortifying breath she straightened, disappointed that the big, warm hand rubbing her back was removed.

When she met Major's concerned gaze she swallowed around the unexpected lump of emotion constricting her throat.

"Are you sure you're okay, Delta?" he asked.

She nodded again as she signed, "Fine."

When she shoved to her feet Major rose as well. She hadn't even noticed that Ace and Rocco had moved away, and when she glanced over at them, tears of gratitude burned the back of her eyes, but she quickly blinked them away. The two men had already mopped up the water and were both heading toward the kitchen.

She spun on her heels to follow them so she could thank them and was surprised again, when Major gripped her elbow so she wouldn't end up on her ass once more.

When she entered the kitchen, Ace and Rocco had already dumped the water and put the mop and bucket to the side.

She shifted her gaze to Major. "Thank you all so much for your help. I really appreciate it."

Major smiled down at her, his gray-blue eyes twinkling. "You're welcome, honey. Since we're here, why don't you let us help you finish up?"

"Oh, um, that's okay. I'm sure you have things of your own to do."

Major shook his head. "No, we're free for the night." He eyed her up and down, and the light in his eyes changed to what she didn't know. When she glanced down, she gasped when she realized her soaked white shirt was transparent. The lacy red bra stuck out like a sore thumb and the top of her breasts were easily visible.

Delta quickly lifted her arms and crossed them over her chest as she gazed back up at Major again. "Do you have a change of clothes with you?"

"Yes. I live upstairs."

"Why don't you go take a shower and get into some dry clothes, honey? By the time you come back down, we'll have everything done."

Delta wasn't sure she wanted to leave three men she'd just met down in her diner while she went upstairs to clean up. It wasn't that she thought they'd steal from her or do anything bad, she just wasn't used to being around other people all that much. Dealing with customers and this…situation was totally different.

The question that had been plaguing her from the second she saw all three men in her diner burst rapidly across her fingers. "How did you all get in here?"

Major frowned. "We opened the door and walked in. Why?"

"Cindy always locks the door as she leaves."

"Maybe she forgot," he said.

Delta nodded as she glanced toward the kitchen door. Cindy was always diligent about locking up after her since the young woman knew she was here alone. A knot of anxiety started to form in her gut. There was no way she would be able to settle unless she checked the door herself. She turned and headed back out into the diner and straight for the entrance. When she grabbed the handle, and turned it, it opened easily. She closed it again and flicked the lock over and then tugged on the handle again. A shiver of apprehension raced up her spine. The lock had worked fine the previous night. Why wouldn't it be working now?

Major tapped her on the shoulder and she startled. He clasped her upper arms in his hands to steady her and then guided her to the side of the door and released her. He bent over and studied the lock, turning it around and back again. Then he went down on bended knee and peered at it closely. Delta had no idea what he was staring at, but when he gazed at her from over his shoulder, she saw a hard, angry look in his eyes.

She took a few steps back as fear once more skittered up her spine. Major held his hands up, palms facing her as he got back to his feet.

"Don't be afraid of me, honey. Ace, Rocco, and I would never do anything to hurt you."

The tension eased from her muscles and the slight adrenaline surge began to wane. She glanced from him to the door and raised an eyebrow in query.

The next words he signed to her had the fear surging back to life.

"Someone's tampered with the lock."

"What? Why?"

"I don't know, Delta." The muscles in the side of his jaw ticked as he ground his teeth. She didn't understand what he had to be upset about since it was her door. "Most of the screws have been removed from the door. The one holding the latch in place has been stripped of its thread."

"What does that mean?" she asked.

"It means that the door can't be locked. It means that anyone could walk in here in the middle of the night or whenever they wanted."

Delta had no idea what to do. The thought of being so vulnerable had terror coursing through her blood. She had no idea why anyone would have any interest in her, would want to get to her, but that's exactly what it looked like.

She didn't know anyone except Cindy and now Carly, as well as Major and his brothers. Carly, Major, Rocco, and Ace were still all strangers to her, and although she was skittish around most people, she felt as if she could trust the Porter men and Carly.

Major moved closer to her. "You can't stay here, honey. It's not safe."

"This is my home," Delta signed quickly, glad that anger was replacing the fear. "I'm not letting anyone run me out of my home."

"I understand, Delta, but you could be putting your life on the line. Are you willing to do that just to save a building?"

"This"—she waved her hand around toward the diner—"isn't just a building. It's my livelihood. My lifeblood. My dream. I'll be fine. There's a deadlock to the door leading to the upstairs apartment."

"Show me," Major commanded.

Delta was still angry but with a nod, she turned and headed out through the diner, into the hallway, past the kitchen and to the door that led to her upstairs apartment. She pointed and stepped aside so he could see the lock. He tried to turn the handle, but since she always locked it when she came down first thing in the morning, it didn't budge. He glanced toward the rear entrance to the diner, brushed by her and opened the door.

"Why isn't this door locked?" Major asked.

"It should be," she replied. Goosebumps rose over her skin as Major once more studied the deadbolt.

"You can't stay here," he said over his shoulder and then he stood and faced her.

"I have to." Her voice would have risen with agitation if she'd been able to speak. "I have a delivery first thing and food preparation to see to."

"What time do you need to be down here?"

Delta didn't want to tell him she had to get up at four in the morning because she had a feeling he wouldn't be very happy about it, so instead of answering, she shrugged. There so much still left to do tonight, she didn't have the time to be dilly dallying the time away. Before Major could grill her some more, she hurried back toward the kitchen. Tears pricked the back of her eyes when she saw that Rocco and Ace had scrubbed and dried all the pots and pans and were just unloading the last things from the dishwashers.

They both straightened and smiled at her as she walked farther into the room. "Thank you."

Rocco nodded and Ace's grin widened.

Delta turned toward the fridge, hoping if she ignored the three handsome men, they'd get tired of being around her and leave.

Chapter Three

Rocco glanced from Major to Delta and back to his brother again. He could see by the way Major's fists were clenched and the way the muscles in his jaw were flexing that something was wrong.

"What's going on?" Ace asked before he could.

Major watched the beautiful woman pull her hair up onto the top of her head before she washed her hands. Delta then began to pull ingredients from the fridge, carry them to the large counter, and start chopping. He sighed as he rubbed the back of his neck. "Someone's tampered with the lock on the front and back door to this place."

"What the fuck?" Rocco asked angrily. "Who the fuck would want to do that?"

"The more important question is, why?" Ace barked the last word.

"I don't know, and I'm not sure Delta does either, but she's scared."

"Of course she is. What woman on her own wouldn't be?" Rocco asked rhetorically. He couldn't keep his gaze from Delta even though her back was turned to them. She was so fucking gorgeous. She was of average height, and had the sexiest hour glass figure he'd ever had the privilege of seeing. Delta was slim with pert breasts, a narrow waist, and curvy hips. Although she wasn't overly tall, her legs were long and toned. He'd seen her cargo shorts pulled tight over her sexy ass and wanted to see if those peachy globes would fit into his hands as perfectly as they looked as if they would. Her light blonde hair was slightly wavy and hung down below her shoulders. It was also kinked at the back as if she'd just released it from a ponytail or bun or something. He loved the gold blonde streaks in the strands that hung down beside her cheeks. Her skin was pale and looked as smooth as silk and he'd had to resist the urge to find out for himself.

The moment he'd swept her up into his arms earlier had been the moment he knew she was the right woman for him and his brothers. From the way they were acting around her, he suspected Major and Ace felt the same as he did.

However, it wasn't just her beauty or sexy body that drew him, but nor was it because she had a disability. There was just something so sweet about her, and while he figured she was independent, there was an underlying vulnerability about her, too.

"Do either of you know anything about her?" Major asked.

Rocco gave him a look.

Major sighed. "Yeah, I know dumb question since we've all just met her, but I was hoping you might have heard something other than what an amazing cook she is."

"You know as much as we do, bro," Ace said.

"What he said." Rocco pointed at Ace. "We can't leave her here all alone. Not if someone has plans to break in or something else. Did you ask her to come stay at our place?"

"No, I didn't get around to it," Major answered. "I told her she couldn't stay here and she got pissed."

"Fuck, Major. Saying something like that was like waving a red flag in front of a bull. Even you would baulk at being told what to do by someone you don't know." Ace scrubbed a hand over his face.

"He'd baulk at anyone telling him what to do even if he'd known them for years." Rocco smirked.

"We all would," Ace said.

"Let me try." Rocco turned from his brothers and walked toward Delta.

"Knock yourself out," Major muttered.

Rocco moved to stand on the other side of the food prep area and knew Delta could see him when her shoulders tensed, but she didn't stop dicing the bell peppers until he reached toward her.

She met his gaze, blinked and licked her lips before looking at his lips. He had a spontaneous urge to smile, but didn't. He didn't want Delta thinking he was laughing at her. "We're worried about your safety since you live alone and someone's damaged the locks on the front and rear door to the diner. We have a spare bedroom if you'd like to come and stay at our place for the night."

When she didn't react other than continue frowning at him, Rocco wondered if he'd spoken too quickly for her to follow on. He cursed his inability to sign so she could understand him. Right now, he wished he'd learned to sign along with Major when he'd come across a deaf kid while on one of their missions. Since they'd never encountered anyone else that had been hearing impaired, Rocco hadn't seen the point. Now he wished he could turn back time and learn right along with Major. From the wistful expression on Ace's face, his younger brother was berating himself for his previous decision. Nonetheless, all that mattered right now was that they keep Delta safe. He would spend whatever free time he had learning to sign from Major whenever he could.

Delta exhaled noisily, shook her head and mouthed, "Thank you."

Rocco wasn't bothered by her negative answer. He'd already decided that if she refused then he and his brothers would be staying here with her, even if it meant he had to sleep in the truck.

He met Ace's and then Major's gazes. "Looks like we're staying here the night. Which one of you wants to go home and get a change of clothes?"

"We won't need any," Major said. "We don't all need to lose sleep. Why don't you two go home. I'll stay and keep her safe."

Rocco moved back over toward his brothers, just in case Delta looked up when he was speaking. He didn't want her getting pissed at them when she realized they were talking about her. "We all want to spend time with her, Major."

"I know, but if we all stay here, she's going to be more wary than she already is. We don't want her to feel too crowded. She doesn't know us from Adam. Rocco, you're going to have slow down. You're always rushing where women are concerned, but we need to go at Delta's pace if we want to win her affection."

"You don't need to fucking tell me how to handle a woman, Major. I wasn't born yester-fucking-day."

"Calm the hell down, Rocco," Ace stated calmly. "She's looking over here and she's frowning."

Rocco nodded and ground his teeth together. As much as he hated to admit it, Major was right. She'd already gone into a panic when he and his brothers had crowded around her earlier.

"What time do you want us to pick you up?" Ace asked as he slapped Rocco on the shoulder, obviously seeing that he'd conceded.

"Six should be early enough," Major said.

Rocco nodded and headed toward the door with Ace right behind him. He paused and looked back over his shoulder at Delta. She had her gaze down and she was chopping again. He met Major's gaze. "Call if you need anything."

"Will do."

Rocco glanced at their woman one more time before leaving, and hoped like hell that Major didn't do or say anything to her that would ruin their chances of wooing her.

* * * *

When Delta noticed the tension in the air was a little lighter, she glanced over her shoulder at Major to see him leaning back against the sink with his arms folded over his chest. Butterflies started fluttering in her belly, and her sex grew slick with moisture. Goosebumps raced over her skin, but she put that down to the soaked clothes she was still wearing. She hadn't bothered to change since it was likely she would just end up with another lot of soiled clothes to wash. However, she'd taken the time to pull a full apron over her head and tie around her waist.

Major was staring at her avidly and while her usual instinct was to lower her gaze and turn away, she didn't. She put the knife she was holding down on the carving board and turned to face him. "What?"

"Nothing," he replied. "I was just wondering how long you were going to be."

She sucked in a breath when she glanced at the clock to see it was almost eleven. While the brothers had been talking behind her back, she'd used the last of the adrenaline and anger still flooding her system to prepare all the vegetables and salads for the next day. The meat and chicken were already marinating and defrosting in the fridge, so thankfully there wasn't much left to do.

Tomorrow morning was another story. She would have to be up at four to stew apples for her apple pies and make the pastry. She had also decided to make a few batches of muffins, and that all needed to be done before the delivery driver arrived at six. She covered the bowls of food with cling wrap and carried them toward one of the industrial sized fridges to refrigerate overnight. Once that was done, she gathered the tools she used and carried them to the sink to wash them. Major grabbed a clean dishtowel and dried the few things while she wiped the counter down.

"I'm done," she said. "Thanks again for all your help. I really appreciate it."

"You don't have to keep thanking me or my brothers, honey. We like to help out."

She nodded. "We'll I'm heading to bed. I'm sure you won't mind seeing yourself out. Will you?"

"I'm not going anywhere, Delta."

"What?"

Major palmed her cheeks with his hands. "You don't think I'm going to leave you here all alone when someone could be out to hurt you, do you?"

She tried to keep the fear from her eyes but knew she'd failed when he frowned. She drew away from him, not because she was frightened of him, but because she liked having his skin, his warmth against her. "I don't know anyone. Who'd want to hurt me?" She rubbed her arms trying to warm her chilled skin. "You're probably overreacting. The lock screws might have worked their way out, since the door gets used so much during the day. Or maybe they were already missing and today was the day the latch decided to fail."

"Don't lie to me, honey. I don't like being lied to."

"What do you want from me?" Delta cried in her head as she signed quickly.

"Everything," Major replied instantly.

She gulped when his gray-blue eyes heated before they eyed her body over and then lifted up to hers again. Her breathing escalated and her heart pounded against her rib cage. When his tongue swept over his lower lip, she stared mesmerized and wondered if he tasted as good as he looked. But when he took a step closer, she shut her thoughts down and stepped back, shaking her head. "That's not possible."

"Why?"

"I don't know you."

"You're right. You don't, but my brothers and I would like the chance to spend some time with you.

"I can't. I don't have time. I have a diner to run. I'm hardly keeping my head above water as it is. You and your brothers will just complicate things."

"What are you so scared of, Delta?"

She scoffed, or hoped she did. "I'm not scared of anything. All I want is to be left alone to run my business in peace."

There was a flash of something in his eyes, but it was gone so quickly she couldn't discern what it was, but when he nodded and crossed his arms over his chest again, she sighed with relief. There was no way that sigh was of despondency. At least that's what she told herself.

"I'm still staying the night. I couldn't live with myself if something happened. I'm going to call the sheriffs and get them out to take a look at the locks, maybe even dust for prints. Don't worry, I won't encroach on your privacy. Lock the stairway door and go and get some sleep."

From the implacable expression on Major's face he wasn't going to back down or change his mind no matter how much she argued, so she didn't bother to try and sway his decision and headed out. "Thank you," she signed and then left.

* * * *

"What's going on?" Luke Sun-Walker, one of the Slick Rock sheriffs asked as he got out of his car. Damon Osborn, another sheriff got out of the passenger seat.

Major shook both men's hands. "The locks to the back and front door of the diner have been interfered with."

"Shit! Is Delta all right?" Damon asked.

"Yeah, I think so. She's gone upstairs."

"You stayed to keep her safe?" Luke asked.

"I did. There was no way in hell I was leaving her alone while she was so vulnerable."

"What were you doing here so late anyway?" Damon asked from his squat position near the lock on the front door.

"We were worried and curious," he answered honestly.

"Worried, why?" Luke asked.

"Did you know she's only got one waitress working for her?"

"Yeah," Luke replied angrily. "I'm going to the high school tomorrow morning. All the students have been called to an assembly and I'm going to read them the riot act."

"How can people be so narrow-minded?" Major asked.

"From what I've gathered there are only a few prejudiced students," Damon interjected as he stood.

Major followed him and Luke through the diner toward the back door. "Then why hasn't any applied for jobs here."

"Circumstances," Luke said. "School's just back from summer break. The kids are getting into the swing of things, and our new diner owner is very reclusive. She doesn't even go out to the supermarket to get supplies. No one knows who she is, or what she even looks like. You know how small towns work."

"I think Luke's right," Damon said. "People want to know who they're going to be working for. The people in this town are very liberated in the way they think. They've had to be after Clay and Johnny Morten stood up to them when they found their wife, Tara, when the first ménage was formed."

"Delta's reclusive, and while she might have good reason to be so, that's not going to help her find employees." Luke scowled as he stood up straight. "Someone's definitely fucked with these locks. Damon, can you dust them for prints?"

"I can, but I don't think it will help. A lot of people will have touched these locks."

Luke nodded. "I think we should call Giles, Remy, and Brandon Alcott. Get them to set up a state of the art security system with cameras, alarms, new deadlocks. The whole works."

Major wasn't leaving Delta's safety to chance. The moment he'd set his gaze on her when she came out the mop the diner floor was etched into his mind for all time.

His heart had stopped beating when she'd first come into view before slamming hard against his sternum. He'd had trouble catching his breath and his cock had gone from flaccid to full attention within a few seconds, leaving him light headed. He'd never reacted so quickly to a woman in his life. She was so fucking beautiful he had to work at keeping his desire for her under wraps, especially when he and his brothers had raced inside to help her. Being close to her was so damned amazing. He'd wanted to pull her into his arms and never let go.

He and his brothers were going to need to curb their excitement as well as their enthusiasm and lust. He didn't want Delta turning away from them. Major's aim was to wear her down little by little until she agreed to spend time with him and his brothers, and if that took months, then they'd just have to be patient.

He loved seeing her blonde wavy hair streaming down around her shoulders and had nearly moaned out loud when she'd pulled her hair back up and out of her face. Her eyes were the most mesmerizing jade green and he would have been happy staring into their depths for the rest of his life. She wasn't like other chefs he'd seen wearing the white uniform of their profession. She wore firm black cargo shorts with a white blouse and covered her clothes with an apron while she'd been working with the food.

He'd nearly fallen to his knees when he'd seen the racy, red lace bra under her wet shirt and had to work at keeping his eyes locked with hers after his initial glimpse of those soft, luscious globes.

Major frowned as he tried to figure out why she hadn't gone upstairs to change out of her soaked clothes. Her gaze had skittered away from his and then she'd just ignored his suggestion. She had to have been damned cold and uncomfortable working in such a state. It took a few moments for the penny to drop. She wasn't used to being around a lot of people, and if he hazarded a guess, men even less than women.

Delta seemed to be rather reclusive and he had a feeling it had to do with her hearing impairment. Major tried to imagine what it would be like to go through life without being able to hear or speak like other people did. Other humans could be so damn cruel to someone a little different from the norm, and he hoped like hell she hadn't been subjected to cruelty at others' hands, but knew she had. If he'd been kept on the outside looking in because of a disability, he might have been reclusive, too.

He mentally shook his head. No, that wasn't him at all. Major and his brothers didn't give a fuck about what other people thought. They would have continued on enjoying life and doing what they wanted no matter what.

So, what had made Delta so introverted?

That was a question he was determined to have the answer to.

"Giles and Remy are on their way," Damon said, bringing Major from his introspections.

"Thank you. I appreciate it."

"Just doing our jobs." Damon offered his hand to Major.

He shook his hand and then Luke's and walked them out to their vehicle.

Damon held up the fingerprints he'd collected from the locks, which were now sealed in a plastic bag. "If I find anything, I'll let you know."

"Thanks, guys."

Once the sheriffs left, Major headed back inside to wait for Remy and Giles. He'd only met the Alcott men once and had liked them on sight. He just hoped they weren't too pissed to be pulled out of their beds and away from their wife in the middle of the night, but suspected they wouldn't.

The men in Slick Rock were all about protecting the fairer sex and making sure they were safe, no matter what time of day or night it was.

Major just hoped that Delta didn't get pissed when she found out he'd upgraded her security system.

Chapter Four

It had been easy to follow that deaf slut from Chicago to the small backward town of Slick Rock. His brother had died because of that bitch and he was going to do everything he could to make sure she paid. Larry had been Leo's only living relative and now his brother was gone.

He'd never forgotten the pain of finding out his brother's life had been snuffed out in the blink of an eye. He'd heard it on the radio that fateful morning months ago, and had vowed then and there to extract retribution.

Leo had even gone to the hospital to find out who the bitch was, but the fucking nurses had been closed up tighter than a nun in a chastity belt. Thankfully, the media had gotten hold of the information he'd wanted and reported the cunt's name over the air just for him. However, since he'd been working on a construction site on the other side of town, he'd only had afterhours to case her joint. Somehow the cunt had been able to pack up and leave town before he could make his move. It hadn't been hard to track her down since her name wasn't common, and when he'd found she'd registered a new business in Slick Rock, Colorado, he'd followed.

Getting work and an apartment to rent had been a breeze since the town was booming. He was now working for Trent and Tristan Woodall. They seemed like decent enough guys, and when Leo had found out they were also owners of the only bank in town with their older brother, Trick, he began to think that maybe he should follow in his brother's footsteps.

Maybe if Larry had taken time to scope out the bank and plan, he might have gotten away with a shit load of money, and they both would have been sitting pretty for the rest of their lives. He could just imagine Larry and him sunning themselves on lounge beds under the hot sun on a tropical island, sipping some exotic alcoholic drinks, but now Larry would never see the light of day again.

Leo had been in town for just over two months now. Yesterday he'd been able to damage the locks on the diner just after the doors opened before the breakfast rush. He'd been able to break the locks on the front and back doors with plans to come back in the early hours of the next morning to kill that bitch, but his plans had been thwarted. He hadn't expected the cow to find the broken locks and call in someone to fix them that night.

He'd driven to the diner just after two in the morning and had been shocked to find the place lit up like a Christmas tree. As he'd driven by he'd cursed when he'd seen the logo of the local security company on one of the trucks parked out the front. From what he'd heard, Alcott Security was one of the best of the best in the country.

Leo headed back home. He was going to have to make new plans if he was going to get vengeance. He would think of something and when he did, that slut was toast.

* * * *

Delta groaned when her cell phone vibrated under her cheek. She'd thought about getting one of those flashing alarm clocks that was specifically made for deaf people, but hadn't bothered. She'd accidentally fallen asleep with her phone under her pillow when she'd been a teenager, and the phone had vibrated when she'd received an incoming text and awoken her. So, from then on, she'd made sure the alarm clock on her cell was set on vibrate whenever she needed to be up at a certain time. Worked like a charm, but she was so tired, today she wished she could just turn the infernal thing off, roll over and go back to sleep. However, since there was so much to do before she opened the diner's door, she didn't have that luxury.

She made quick work of showering and dressing before heading downstairs, flipping lights on as she went. Her first task was to get a pot of fresh coffee brewing, which she did and while she waited for her first cup of the heart-starting brew, she began to get ingredients out of the massive walk in pantry for the muffins she planned to make.

When she turned toward the kitchen counter, she got the fright of her life. She thought she may have screamed since she felt her throat vibrate and the container of flour in her hands went tumbling toward the floor. Major was fast on his feet and caught the flour before it hit and made a huge mess. Delta pressed a hand over her racing heart and she drew in deep breaths of air.

"Sorry," Major signed after placing the container on the counter. "I didn't mean to scare you. I thought you knew I was here."

She shook her head. "I thought you left last night."

It was Major's turn to shake his head. "I couldn't leave you unprotected."

Even though his signed words made her heart swell with warmth, she didn't let it show. Or hoped she didn't. Nonetheless she did thank him. "Thank you for making sure I was safe, but there was no need."

"There was every need," Major replied, his eyes firm with resolve.

She crossed her arms beneath her breasts when he turned his back to her and headed for the freshly brewed coffee. She watched with frustration as he searched out a couple of mugs and then filled them both before turning back to hand her one of the steaming mugs. She couldn't seem to stop herself from watching his lips as they pursed and he blew across the surface of the steaming liquid before taking a sip. When she realized she was staring at his mouth, she lowered her gaze to her own drink and hoped her cheeks weren't as flushed as they felt. She watched him from beneath lowered lashes as he placed his cup down on the counter and took a step toward her. She lifted his gaze to hers and frowned when he beckoned her to follow him.

She trailed after him into the brightly lit diner and gasped when she saw two men packing up what looked like tools and some sort of electrical equipment. She frowned as she brought her gaze back to Major's. "What's going on? Who are these men?"

"Delta, I'd like you to meet Giles and Remy Alcott. Guys, this is Delta Sykes, the new diner owner."

Both men smiled and nodded at her. Giles moved closer holding his hand out in her direction. "Pleased to meet you."

"You, too," she signed, aware that Major was interpreting for her, when she saw his lips moving from the corner of her eye.

"Hi, Delta," Remy said as he shook her hand. He then turned to gaze at Major. "You're all set. Do you need us to hang around and show Delta how things work?"

"No, I've got it," Major replied.

While she had no idea what they were talking about, Delta was glad that Major was signing everything that was said, including her in the conversation, even if she was utterly clueless.

The two Alcott brothers nodded at them before leaving.

"What's going on?" Delta asked.

"I ordered you a state of the art security system."

"You what? I can't afford something like that," Delta signed angrily.

"Slow down, baby. I can't keep up."

She blew out a frustrated breath and repeated what she'd just said.

Major moved closer, cupping her cheeks in his hands. He pressed a soft kiss to her forehead, shocking her into immobility before he drew back and started signing. "You don't have to worry about the cost. Me, Rocco, and Ace have it covered."

"You had no right!"

"I had every right!" Major gave her a fierce look of determination. "Do you think I could honestly live with my conscience if I didn't see to your protection? I'm not about to let some fucker walk in here and hurt what's mine."

The hackles on her nape rose on end. "I'm not yours. I'm not a fucking pet to be told what to do, or be led around on a leash."

"No, you're not." Major took another step toward her.

Delta had to suppress the shudder from showing as the heat of his big, brawny body seeped into hers. Before she could think of anything else to say, he hooked an arm around her waist and pulled her tight up against him. This time she couldn't contain the shiver from quaking up her smaller frame.

His hand cupped the back of her neck and he nuzzled her neck with his nose, right under her ear. She felt the vibrations of her voice and realized she'd moaned. Delta planted her hands on his toned pecs intending to push away, to create some space between them, but she didn't get the chance. He caressed the side of her throat with his fingers and tilted her chin up with his thumb gently pressing on the underside. She blinked with shock as the muscles in her body, in her legs, seemed to melt and she felt as if she was in danger of falling to the floor. Just as she locked her knees in place, his mouth opened over hers.

Heat.

Delta had never felt such heat in her life. He was as hot as an electric blanket, his warmth chasing away the cold she hadn't realized she'd been carrying around inside of her. She couldn't believe he was kissing her. His lips brushing back and forth against hers felt so amazingly good, she couldn't help but yearn for more.

This was her first kiss. Ever. She'd never let anyone get close enough to touch her let alone kiss her. The breath backed up in her lungs exploded out in a rush from between her parted lips. When his warm moist tongue swept over her bottom lip and then delved inside she was lost.

Major tasted so good. Coffee mixed in with the spiciness of a sexy man. She inhaled through her nose and her chest vibrated on a groan when she was assailed by his delectable spicy scent. He smelled so good, so right, she wanted to keep inhaling his fragrance over and over.

She was lost in him, his heat, his passion, his taste. She was only vaguely aware of a cool breeze brushing over her exposed skin, but was too intent on savoring her first kiss to think about it.

His tongue rubbed along and then swirled around hers. Major licked and sucked on her lips and her tongue before delving in deep again. Delta could have gone on kissing him forever, but a flash of alarm rang inside of her head. She shouldn't be doing this. She was here to run a business, not get involved with one or more men. There was and never would be any room in her life for a relationship. She wasn't about to set herself up to get her heart broken. No one wanted a flawed woman in their life. This was just lust on his part. If she gave him what he wanted—into her pants like every other man she'd ever met—he would no doubt turn and walk away without a qualm.

Delta turned her head and broke the kiss, and shoved against his chest. He released her straight away and she spun on her heels, keeping her gaze lowered, intending to get back to work. She hit a brick wall.

Hands grasped her waist, steadying her, and when she looked up, heat suffused her cheeks when she met Rocco's heated gray-green gaze. When she went to lower her gaze with embarrassment, he wouldn't let her. He clasped her chin between his finger and thumb. "Are you okay?" he asked.

She nodded, shoving his hand from her face at the same time and hurried toward the kitchen. Tears of embarrassed humiliation burned her eyes but she wasn't about to let them fall. She'd learned at a very young age that crying never solved anything.

Her father had abandoned her and her mom when she'd found out she was pregnant. From what she could remember, her mom had been a wonderful woman, but she'd died when Delta was just five years old. She'd been put into an institution for the deaf and blind, and even though she'd been surrounded by other people, she'd always felt so alone.

The teachers and care workers at the institute had been wonderful, teaching all the kids how to deal with a disability and how to get on in life, but Delta had missed her mom so much, she'd shut down emotionally. That had been her survival mechanism. It had saved her a lot of angst time and time again. Even though sometimes, she wished she could be more open and friendly, especially since there was so much prejudiced in the world against someone a little different. She'd been segregated her whole life and couldn't see that changing anytime soon.

She was mixing a large batch of muffin mix when the three men entered the kitchen, but she kept her gaze lowered and ignored them. That was, until the bowl and spoon were snatched from her hands and set aside. She scowled at Ace but he ignored her pique, grabbed her hand, and led her back out into the diner.

After releasing her hand, he clasped her face between his hands. "You need to learn how to use and activate the security system, honey."

Delta was tempted to tell these men they could take their security system and shove it where the sun didn't shine, but she was also relieved to have it since she was more than a little worried about the damaged locks. She hadn't believed a word she'd said when she suggested the screws had worked themselves loose to Major last night.

With a sigh of resignation, she nodded and sat down at the table where all the paperwork was strewn. Major and Rocco sat across from her while Ace took the seat next to her.

It took over half an hour for them to explain how to use the system, and though she was appreciative, she was also aware of how quickly time was ticking by.

Finally, when the three men rose, she did, too. "Thank you for staying last night and making sure I was safe." She locked gazes with

Major while she signed, then shifted her gaze to first Ace and Rocco. "Thank you, all of you for the security system. It may take a while, but I will pay you back."

Ace and Rocco smiled and nodded at her. Major frowned as he signed, "You're welcome. I've written our cell numbers down for you. If you ever need anything, please don't hesitate to contact us."

Delta nodded. "Thanks again."

The three men turned toward the door and left without a backward glance. That made her think she was right to not get involved with one of more of the Porter men. They were only being nice to her so they could get her into their beds. Once they had what they wanted, she had no doubt she'd never see them again.

* * * *

"What the fuck were you thinking?" Rocco snarled as soon as he and his brothers were in the truck heading back to their ranch. He was in the driver's seat with Ace sitting next to him in the passenger seat and Major in the back. He glanced in the rearview mirror to see Major scrubbing a hand down his face.

"I wasn't thinking at all," Major finally replied.

"You're damn fucking right you weren't. You're a fucking hypocrite, Major. Last night you were the one telling me to take things slow with her and what do we find when we come to pick you up? You have your fucking tongue half way down her throat."

"Calm the fuck down, Rocco," Ace said angrily. "What's done is done and there's no changing it."

Rocco gripped the steering wheel so tight, his knuckles were white and his hands started aching. He was going to have the imprint of the wheel in his skin for the next few hours.

"I know I fucked up," Major said. "I don't even remember thinking about kissing her until my lips were on hers."

"Don't beat yourself up, bro," Ace said as he gazed over his shoulder. "She was kissing you back just as hungrily as you were kissing her there for a while."

"She was, wasn't she?" Major chuckled.

"Asshole." Rocco smiled at him in the mirror. "Does she taste as good as you imagined, as sweet as she looks?"

"No. Way fucking better."

"So, what do we do now?" Rocco asked.

"We go to the diner as often as we can," Major answered.

"Do you think someone is after her?" Ace frowned.

"I don't know, but it sure as hell looks like it. Why would someone tamper with the locks otherwise?"

"The question is who?" Rocco asked as he checked the mirrors, indicated, and changed lanes.

"There are a lot of single men in and around Slick Rock," Ace said. "Could be anyone."

"That doesn't make sense." Rocco checked both ways before turning onto the road leading to their ranch. "If members of the opposite sex were interested in Delta, they would have asked her out."

"Not necessarily," Ace said.

"Ace is right," Major agreed. "There are a lot of new people in and around town. People have moved away from the cities for a slower paced life. Those two new housing estates have sold like hot cakes, and the third estate is nearly ready to be put on the market."

"The sheriffs were going to check into everyone new in town." Rocco slowed as he turned into the driveway.

"I have no doubt they will, but there are only so many hours in a day. The sheriffs and deputies are out patrolling, or attending car accidents on the highway, as well as the normal shit they have to deal with day in day out. Doing background checks on the new residents of Slick Rock will be put on the backburner until they have some spare time."

Rocco grunted in acknowledgement to Major's statement. His brother was right, the sheriffs had a lot on their plate. Crime was on the rise in town with burglaries and other misdemeanors. Background checks would be the least of the Sheriff Department's concerns.

He headed toward the barn and the horses. After he tacked up his gelding, mounted up and headed out to the far eastern pasture. The cattle needed to be moved to another paddock where there was more feed. Ace and Major would join him soon enough, but Rocco was so agitated he was glad for a few minutes alone.

He'd never wanted a woman the way he wanted Delta, and while he envied Major getting to kiss her, he was also still pissed at him. If his older brother had fucked up their chances with the gorgeous Delta, he wasn't sure he'd ever be able to forgive him. Especially after Major had told him to be careful with her and then gone and done the opposite himself.

He also wanted to help with hiring waitstaff for her, but after he'd seen the anger in her stunning green eyes over the security system, Rocco didn't think any more help from him and his brothers would go over well.

He hoped that Carly and Cindy could get the other women in Slick Rock on board with them so Delta could get the help she needed.

Chapter Five

Please, please, please, Delta mentally chanted. She was begging anyone who would listen for more staff. If it had helped any, she would have gotten down on her knees and prayed to every single god she'd ever heard of.

Just before the lunch rush started, Cindy entered the diner's kitchen and beckoned her out to the dining area. The young girl was smiling from ear to ear and while Delta found herself smiling as well, she had no idea why.

When she spotted Carly sitting at a booth in the back with a stack of papers in front of her, and a group of women and girls waiting in line, she realized what was going on. Carly was interviewing waitstaff for her. Tears of gratitude welled, and while she tried to blink them back one escaped over the rim and rolled down her cheek. Carly must have heard her coming or maybe Cindy had called her name because the other woman, stood and turned to face her. She was smiling smugly.

Delta glanced at Cindy when she tapped her on the arm.

"Carly and her friends have spent the morning interviewing, and with your approval they've chosen five girls who would love to work with you," Cindy explained. "This is Enya. She's been working for a bakery and has a pastry chef's college degree. She moved to Slick Rock two days ago."

Delta nodded in greeting.

Cindy pointed to another young woman who smiled and waved at her. "This is Jaylynn. The twins in the back are Katie and Kiara, and last but not least, is Lilac."

"Are you sure they're all happy to work here?" Delta asked.

"Yes," Cindy replied. "Katie and Kiara have just graduated from high school. They were smart enough to finish a year early and while they both have scholarships to go to college, they've deferred a year to save up some money. Their mom is sick and they're looking after her.

"Lilac is new to town and saw the help wanted sign in the window. She came in straight away. She's from Minnesota and is used to being on her feet, and she's worked in a well-known restaurant in New York City," Cindy explained.

"Please tell them all thank you, and I look forward to working with and getting to know them all."

Cindy turned to the new waitstaff and passed on Delta's gratitude. Once she was done, she turned to face Carly and her friends and starting signing. "Carly, ladies, I would like to thank you all so very much for helping me out when things were looking so bad. I will never be able to repay you for what you've done, but the least I can do is give you lunch on the house."

Carly and her friends clapped and smiled, and Delta thought one of them may have whistled since she'd pursed her lips. All five of her new employees shook her hand and then walked toward the serving counter. Cindy had rushed toward the back and returned moments later with aprons, order pads and pencils.

Delta thanked everyone one more time and headed back to the kitchen with a smile on her face. Her silent prayers had been answered. She was happy and her heart was filled with warmth. For the first time in months she felt as if she'd made the right decision by moving to Slick Rock and fulfilling her passion for cooking. These people were almost strangers to her but they had opened their hearts to her without knowing who she was. The least she could do was try and do the same.

Things were finally looking up and she was going to embrace her new life and the wonderful, kind people reaching out to her.

* * * *

Leo watched the women in the back from beneath the brim of his ball cap. One of the ladies was interviewing waitstaff, and while he admired her willingness to help, he was also angry at her. If the dumb cunt had more people working for her it was going to be harder than ever to get his hands on the bitch.

He'd been trying to blend in and thought he was doing a damn good job of it since no one had paid him any attention. Maybe it was because he was wearing one of the construction company's T-shirts and the locals accepted him as a new member of the small town.

When he'd first arrived and seen two or more men walking with one woman, paying her the attention a lover would, he'd thought he stumbled into a cult town. However, he'd kept his ears open and had been shocked to find out there were a lot of ménage relationships around the county. What surprised him the most was how diligent the men were in seeing to their women's comfort. He was going to have to make sure no one was about when he went after that deaf bitch. He'd also seen the upgraded security system when he'd entered the diner, and though he didn't have electrical knowledge he wasn't a total dumbass. Leo knew that a power outage would bring all that fine equipment to a halt.

An idea began to form and it took everything he had not to laugh out loud and draw attention to himself or rub his hands together. He lowered his eyes back to his plate of bacon, eggs, pancakes and syrup. While he hated that slut with a passion, he had to admit she was a damn fine cook. He'd just finished off his last bite when he caught movement from the corner of his eye. The deaf idiot was behind the serving counter signing with one of the young waitresses. He glanced their way from beneath his hat and wondered if he should go after the young waitress. She would be easier to get his hands on than the deaf chick, since she had to come and go to and from work. He could use her to draw the cunt out, but first he was going to have some fun with the slut. By the time he was finished with her, she would be screaming for mercy. He quickly negated the idea of getting his hands on the young girl. It would be harder to grab the waitress, since she could hear. Going after the deaf bitch was his only goal, anyway. He didn't have a beef with the teenage waitress. She was just unfortunate to be working for the bitch.

Leo would make the first move in his game of cat and mouse, and when he made the last move, the deaf cunt would know there was no way in hell she would find any redemption for what she'd done.

* * * *

Usually Ace loved working with the animals out in the open on their ranch, but the day seemed to take way longer to pass than normal. He was itching to get back to the diner so he could see Delta again. Just thinking about her had him semi-hard and it was damned uncomfortable trying to ride his horse when his cock was being strangled by his jeans.

The urge to say, "fuck it" and ignore his chores was strong, but he couldn't. The cattle relied on him and his brothers to make sure they had enough food and water to make it through the hot summer's day.

The minutes dragged as he worked his way through his chores. As soon as Major had entered the house he'd gone straight to bed to catch a few hours of sleep. Rocco had just been entering the barn when Ace rode out. His brother had been going to head toward the east pasture to move the herd of cattle to the paddock next to it so the animals had fresh grazing. The weekend before they gotten some much needed rain, which had ended up lasting three days straight, and while the eastern field still had plenty of feed left, none of them wanted the animals eating it down to the roots. Summer was close to over but the rainfall hadn't been anywhere near what it was supposed to be.

After glancing at his watch for about the hundredth time, Ace, sighed with frustration and scrubbed a hand down his face. If he was going to get through all his work, he needed to get his mind on the task at hand and stop thinking about Delta. Just maybe if he could concentrate long enough he would finish up early, and after cleaning up he and his brothers could head to the diner before the dinner rush. Feeling a little lighter, Ace urged his mount forward, determination giving him a figurative spring in his step.

* * * *

Although she was hot, sweaty and tired, Delta couldn't stop smiling. The day had gone so smoothly with her newly hired staff, she felt like dancing a jig. Enya and Lilac had worked really hard, making sure all the ordered meals were delivered as soon as she placed them under the warming light. They'd cleared tables, poured coffee, taken money and placed orders without a hitch.

Cindy had also served the customers, but the young woman had also kept up with the dishes, making sure plates were scraped, rinsed and put in the dishwasher.

Delta would have hummed the whole day through if she'd been able to. There was a lightness and music in her heart, and while her day wasn't done yet, since the dinner rush hour was just about to start, she was actually able to take a much needed break for a change.

"All the muffins sold within the first two hours," Cindy signed.

Delta nodded and smiled. "I'll have to make sure to triple the next batch." She glanced at Enya as she entered with another tub of dirty dishes and placed them on the counter next to the sink. She glanced at Delta before gazing at Cindy. She could see Enya's lips moving but since the woman was side on to her, Delta didn't know what she was saying.

Cindy waved at her to get her attention. "Enya just told me that she used to make muffins and cakes for a restaurant and the bakery she worked for. She's offering to do the same for the diner. She's a pastry and sous chef."

"For real?" Delta asked excitedly.

Enya turned to face Delta, nodded and smiled. "I love baking. I really miss making muffins and cakes. Will you please let me?"

Delta was excited and couldn't keep the smile from her face. She walked over to Enya and pulled her into her arms. She felt the other woman tense and hoped she hadn't overstepped her personal bounds, but after a couple of seconds, Enya relaxed and hugged her back. She felt the other woman's chest expand and then contract as if she'd just given a big sigh. She finally released her and nodded before she started signing, so happy that she had Cindy to interpret. "I would love it if you would make, muffins, cakes and pies. If you agree, I would love to have you working with me in the kitchen, too."

Enya smiled and nodded. "Yes. I would love that. Thank you."

"It should be me thanking you. So, thank you, so very much."

"You're welcome. What sort of things do you want me to make?"

"Can we work out the details later?" Delta asked. She hurried over to the serving window and peeked out before turning back to face the other women. "The dinner rush is just arriving."

"Sure, and don't hesitate to let me know if you need help." Enya was facing Delta and while Cindy continued to sign she was able to read the other woman's lips.

"I will" She turned toward the oven to check on the two large beef roasts she had slow cooking. The tantalizing smells wafting from the oven had her salivating and her stomach rumbling. She couldn't remember eating anything today, but she was feeling a little jittery since she'd had way too much coffee.

So why the hell was the hair on the back of her neck standing on end? Delta felt as if she was being watched.

* * * *

"That was the best damn roast beef I've ever tasted." Ace patted his belly and leaned back into the seat.

"Yeah." Rocco sighed as he glanced toward the serving window.

Major nodded in agreement. The diner was packed and while he loved that their woman's business was thriving, he didn't like how many single men were sitting around the place. The single men living in Slick Rock were synonymous for zeroing in on single women with the intention of trying to woo them. He and his brothers were going to have to move fast if they wanted a chance at courting Delta. Most of the men in town were good, honest, hard-working guys, and all of them were very protective of the opposite sex.

That didn't mean they were infallible though. The men involved in polyandrous relationships had certain rules they wanted their wives, girlfriends, or significant others to follow. Such as carrying a fully charged cell phone with them wherever they went, and texting to let their men know where they were, when they were leaving or arriving at a destination. It wasn't because the men were controlling or abusive in any way. It was because they liked to know their women were safe. Every single one of the women who were now involved in the ménage relationships had had trouble follow them to town, and even though their men had tried to protect them, some circumstances were just out of their control. He, his brothers, and the other guys hated that their women had suffered in some way or another, and that was one of the reasons they were all so shielding.

None of the guys living in Slick Rock wanted to see a woman or child scared or hurt, and if they could do something about it, they wouldn't hesitate to step in.

"I can't believe what Carly and the other women have accomplished in such a short amount of time, but I'm happy that Delta now has another five women working for her." Ace smiled at the brunette waitress as she hurried past with a tub full of dirty dishes.

"Yeah." Major rubbed at the back of his neck. He loved that their woman had more help, but he hated how busy the place was. How were he and his brothers supposed to court Delta if she was always working?

"Do you think any of the new staff know how to cook?" Ace frowned.

"I fucking hope so," Rocco replied. "Our woman needs to be able to take time off. If she continues to work the way she has been, she'll end up burning out and getting sick."

"We can ask Carly the next time we see her," Ace suggested.

"Good idea." Major nodded. "We have to find a way to have some alone time with her."

"Speak of the angel." Rocco smiled.

Major glanced toward the door. Carly and her husbands, Ridge, Bull, and Rocky had just walked through the door.

Major and his brothers stood to greet their friends. After handshakes to the men and hugs were given to Carly, they sat down again.

"I want to thank you for helping Delta out with the hiring." Rocco reached across the aisle to squeeze Carly's hand.

"You don't need to thank me." Carly smiled. "I hated seeing an injustice done."

Major frowned. "Was there an injustice?"

"Not with the women who are now working here," Carly answered. "Enya and Lilac have only been in town a short while. Katie and Kiara, too. They just moved back home a few days ago."

"Luke and Damon went to the school and talked to the students about discrimination. I think some of the kids were prejudiced, but a few of the girls said their dads didn't want them working for someone they'd never seen," Ridge explained. "No one's ever seen Delta out and about. In fact, she never seems to leave the kitchen."

"I think there's a reason for that," Luke Sun-Walker said.

Major shifted to gaze at the Sheriff. Luke, as well as Clay and Johnny Morten and their wife Tara were standing in the aisle behind the sheriff.

"And what would that be?" Ace asked.

Major waited to hear the answer with bated breath. He'd just been about to ask the same thing, but Ace had beaten him to it.

"That's not my story to tell." Luke frowned as he glanced toward the serving window before turning back to meet his and his brothers' gazes. "Just make sure to take your time with her."

Major knew that was the sheriff's way of saying, "I'll be watching you and if you hurt her, you'll be answering to me". He was glad that Delta had others watching out for her, too, but he also wanted to know what the hell Luke knew.

A knot of dread formed in his stomach. Was their woman in danger like the other women had been?

He was damn well going to find out.

Chapter Six

Delta couldn't believe how well the five new women and Cindy worked together. The kitchen was sparkling, the tables in the dining area had been wiped down, the floor mopped and all the dishes were already put away. What astounded her was that it was just going on eight-thirty.

This would be the first night in months she would be in bed before midnight. Yes, she still had food prep to do for the next day, but that would only take her a couple of hours at most.

She decided then and there that she would pay her staff more than the minimum wage because they had damn well earned it.

Delta couldn't stop smiling as she began to get the ingredients she needed for the next day's meals. Just as she dumped them onto the counter, Enya and Lilac entered the kitchen with Cindy on their heels.

"Katie and Kiara have gone home and will be back to work from the lunch to dinner rush," Cindy explained.

She smiled and nodded. "You should all go home and get some rest. You've been on your feet all day long."

"So have you," Cindy replied as she glanced at the other two women. "Enya isn't the only experienced chef. Lilac was working as head chef in a prestigious restaurant in New York City."

"You were?" Delta asked excitedly. "Which one?"

Her heart flipped inside her chest when Lilac named the most famous restaurant in the US. "Are you kidding me? Why are you here? You could have your own place."

Wariness entered Lilac's gaze as she shifted from foot to foot. Delta saw shadows in the depths of the young woman's violet eyes and decided not to press. She didn't want Enya feeling as if she was being interrogated. She wanted the woman to hang around for as long as possible and maybe, she would ask her and Enya if they wanted to become part owners with her in the future.

Delta was already tired and she knew she couldn't keep going the pace she had been without paying some price. She didn't want to get sick, but for now, she would hold her cards close to her chest, and give the other women time to settle in.

"It doesn't matter why you left," she said. "I'm so glad to have you all working for me."

"Thanks for hiring us." Lilac smiled. She moved toward the food prep area. "What do you want done with this?"

"I'm making lasagna as well as chicken vegetable soup for lunch tomorrow. The left-over beef will be offered in club sandwiches, and tomorrow night will be the usual steak, as well as roast lamb, and the usual burgers and such." Delta took a deep breath when she went a little light headed and hoped she didn't look as pale as she felt. She blinked to clear her blurry vision and wondered if the other women could see the sweat popping out on her brow.

She took a shaky step toward the counter, praying all the while that her knees didn't give out on her. There was too much to do for her to end up sick now. She didn't have the luxury of being laid up in bed. She released the breath in her lungs, inhaled again, and nearly sighed with relief when her vision cleared. She was about to reach for the vegetable peeler and head to the fridge, but darkness enveloped her, pulling her into a deep dark abyss.

* * * *

Ace was getting impatient. He and his brothers had been sitting in the booth for what felt like hours on end. He, Rocco, and Major had helped the new waitresses clean the diner and mop the floors after introducing themselves. At first Enya and Lilac had been wary of them, but Cindy had put the two women at ease. Cindy knew the score about the men in town and how protective they were since she'd lived in town her whole short seventeen years of life, but she was a sweet little thing. Ace had heard rumors that the girl's mother was an alcoholic and as much as he, his brothers and the rest of the men in town wanted to step in and get her momma the help she needed, he knew it would likely be thrown back in their faces. The sad fact was someone who was dependent on drugs or alcohol needed to ask for help when they were ready to kick their habits. Until then, all any of them could do was make sure Cindy and her sister were looked after.

"What's taking so damn long?" Ace snarled.

"Have a little patience, bro," Major said. "The women have only just finished cleaning up. They're probably helping put the kitchen to rights."

"I want to see her." Ace stood and began to pace.

"And you think we don't?" Rocco snapped.

"Shit!" Ace scrubbed a hand over his face. He was about to walk back to the booth and sit down but stopped when he heard a thud.

"Oh God," Cindy said loudly.

Ace didn't hesitate to race toward the kitchen. His heart stopped beating in his chest when he saw Enya and Lilac kneeling on the floor next to a prone Delta.

"What the hell?" Major asked as he and Rocco entered the kitchen.

Ace knelt on the floor next to Delta and checked her pulse. It was strong and steady, but her face was way too pale and her skin had a light sheen of perspiration.

"One minute she was fine, talking and smiling and the next she got real pale. After taking a couple of breaths the color started coming back into her cheeks, but then she all of a sudden collapsed," Cindy explained.

"I don't think she's eaten anything today," Enya said as she met Ace's gaze before gazing back at Delta. "I only saw her drinking coffee and water."

"Do you want me to call the doctor?" Cindy asked.

Rocco helped Enya and Lilac to their feet. Both women hurried over to the other side of the room as if they couldn't stand being near them. Ace frowned over that but he was too worried about Delta to give it much thought.

"I think we should wait a few minutes," Major stated as he crouched on the other side of their woman next to Rocco.

Ace lifted Delta into his arms and rose. "Is there a sofa in the office?"

"Yes." Cindy nodded before leading the way out of the kitchen and down the hallway. She shoved the door open and stepped aside.

Ace moved over to sit on the sofa against the far wall and cradled Delta in his arms. Major and Rocco followed him into the room but stopped a few feet from the furniture. They stood with their arms crossed over their chests and worried frowns on their faces.

Ace didn't like how little she weighed and wondered if she had been skipping too many meals. Or maybe she was one of those women who was always watching her weight. He fucking hoped not. She had no need to worry about something like that. He would be attracted to her even if she was on the heavy side of the scales. The goodness inside of her shone out through her eyes. He didn't have to spend time with her to see that. Her gorgeous green eyes were so expressive, and while she was wary around him and his brothers, he'd caught the flash of desire in those beautiful orbs the previous night when she'd been staring at them.

He pushed his thoughts aside when she sighed and blinked her eyes open. She was so fucking beautiful she took his breath away.

"Are you okay?" Ace asked.

Delta nodded, glanced about the room and then blushed. She tried to sit up but Ace pressed a hand against her shoulder. "Stay where you are, darlin'. I don't want you passing out again."

Delta frowned and then started signing. "What happened?"

"You fainted," Cindy answered after she moved closer. "Did you eat anything today?"

"Um." Delta huffed out a breath and when her cheeks flushed a brighter pink, Ace knew she hadn't.

"Cindy, can you, Enya, and Lilac get Delta something to eat, please?" Major asked, before turning his stern gaze back to their woman.

"Sure," Cindy said before leaving the room.

"Are you trying to make yourself ill?" Major asked.

"No." Delta signed quickly as if she was angry. "I didn't even think about food. It was real busy today. I didn't even realize I hadn't eaten this morning until—"

Ace hated it when Delta sat up and shifted away from him. He wanted to pull her back into his arms and breath in her delectable feminine scent.

"Until what?" Major asked as he squatted down in front of her.

"Until just before I got light headed." Delta sighed with exasperation.

"When was the last time you ate?" Rocco asked.

"Delta?" Major signed.

"What?"

"Rocco asked you a question?"

"Oh. Sorry. Can you repeat that please?" Delta gazed at Rocco's lips

"When was the last time you ate something?" Rocco asked again.

Ace bit his lip when Delta crossed her arms beneath her breasts and glared at Rocco instead of answering. She was so damn sexy when she was being belligerent. Her jade green eyes had lightened in hue, but they were shooting fire at his brother.

"Well?" Rocco breached the gap between them and squatted down in front of Delta, resting his hands on her knees.

She gasped and though she stared down at Rocco's hands for a few seconds, she didn't try to push him away. Ace eyed her body up and down, glad that Enya and Lilac had untied and removed the full apron which she wore to cover her clothes. Sometimes he suspected she used the kitchen and apron as a shield. However, right now there was nothing to hide the way her body was reacting to him and his brothers. Because her arms were crossed beneath her breasts, her white shirt was pulled tight over her chest. The thin material and her bra did nothing to hide the fact that her nipples were hard, and from the way her breathing was escalating she was just as hungry for them as they were for her.

Delta glanced toward him and then shifted her gaze to Major's and back to Rocco's.

Rocco cupped her cheek so she couldn't look away from him again. "Did you have breakfast, honey?"

Ace wanted to shove his brother away from Delta but not because he was jealous. He wanted to lift her back into his arms and lap, but he pushed his impatience aside. If Rocco or Major could get her talking to them, maybe they would be able to get her to agree to spend some time with them.

Delta gnawed on her lip and shook her head. Rocco pulled her lip away from her teeth using his thumb and then brushed it over the lush bow. When Delta shivered, Ace knew then beyond a shadow of a doubt, that she was indeed attracted to him and his brothers. He just hoped that they didn't take too long to make a move on her. If one of the other single men in town snared her up, he didn't think he'd ever be able to forgive his brothers.

"You have to eat regularly, honey. You can't afford to get sick. Okay?" Rocco asked.

Delta nodded and then Ace held his breath. Rocco slowly moved in closer to her with the intent to kiss her. Ace watched her intently hoping like hell she didn't pull away or shove Rocco back. She did neither. She actually surprised him when she placed her hands over his brothers and leaned closer.

The breath exploded from Ace's lungs when Rocco pressed his lips against hers. She made a breathy moaning sound and then she lifted her arms and wrapped them around Rocco's neck.

Rocco hooked his arm around her waist and tugged her ass to the edge of the cushion, situating himself in between her thighs as he shifted from his haunches to his knees. And then he devoured her. Ace was envious of the passionate kisses they shared. He could see Rocco's tongue licking into Delta's mouth and he salivated as he wondered if she tasted as good as she smelled. Even though food aromas clung to her clothes and skin after spending all day long cooking in the diner kitchen, the scents didn't drown out the natural fragrance of her warm, womanly perfume. Delta felt and smelled right to him, and hopefully now that both of his older brothers had made a move on their woman, his turn would be next. However, he didn't want to kiss her in her place of work. He wanted to be able to touch that fire simmering beneath the surface she tried to keep hidden in his own home. He didn't want to chance being interrupted while he was kissing and hopefully, pleasuring his woman. Nonetheless, if he got a chance to taste those lush, full lips, that sexy mouth, he didn't care where he was or who was around. Anything beyond that was for him and his brothers alone. No one was going to see Delta when she was in the throes of a climax, and while they had a long way to go into gentling her to be with them, he wasn't giving up until she was where she was meant to be.

In their house, their beds, and their arms.

* * * *

Rocco couldn't believe he was kissing his woman. He'd dreamed of this since the first time he'd seen her alone in the diner while she'd been mopping the floors, but reality was way fucking better than imagining. She tasted so fucking sweet, he wanted to inhale her, consume her until they were infused into each other's hearts and souls.

He groaned as his tongue slid along and then twirled around hers before sweeping around in her mouth and exploring every inch of her moist cavern. She tasted so good. Like coffee and cookies, ice-cream and apple pie. His hand was so big, or maybe it was because she was so slim, but his large paw spanned nearly her whole lower back. He imagined he'd be able to span her waist with both of his hands without having any problems getting his thumbs to meet.

Delta made a small whimpering sound, and at first, he thought she was about to pull away, but then her arms tightened around his neck and her fingers threaded into his hair. He moaned into her mouth, curled his tongue around hers and drew it into his mouth so he could suckle on it. He lifted his lids to watch her face and was pleased that her eyes were closed and her cheeks were flushed with desire. When she shifted closer he nearly did the unthinkable. How was a man supposed to resist such temptation when all his heart's desires were here, in his arms? She'd widened her legs even more and it took all of his control not to press her back into the sofa and cover her slight body with his larger one. He wanted to shove his hard, aching cock into her wet pussy, but he didn't want to startle her.

Ace could tell she wasn't very experienced with the opposite sex because when they'd first started kissing she'd been tentative as if unsure of what she was doing. However, once the desire took hold and she let her feelings reign, she kissed him back as passionately as he was kissing her.

When she arched her chest into his, he almost lost it. Her hard, little nipples were stabbing into his chest. What he wouldn't give to feel those ripe berries sliding over his naked skin.

He nearly growled with frustration when Major squeezed his shoulder, but Rocco knew this wasn't the most opportune place to start anything. Cindy or one of the other women could enter the office at any moment.

"Ease up, Rocco," Major ordered.

With a sigh of resignation, Rocco slowed the kiss until he was sipping at Delta's lips and then finally lifted his head. Delta removed her arms from around his neck, scooted back on the sofa cushion and then crossed her arms over her breasts.

He wasn't about to let her hide from him, not now that they were just starting to woo her. He clasped her chin in his hand and lifted her gaze to his. "This"—he pointed to himself and his brothers before continuing—"is just the start, honey."

Delta frowned and then glanced toward the door. She shook her head and scooted along the sofa away from him before rising. "I can't do this. It's not right."

Rocco surged to his feet when she turned her back to him and his brothers. Ace shoved from the sofa and came to stand beside him.

"Shit! If you've fucked this up—"

"Don't start," Major snarled at them. "The last thing we need is for Delta to see us fighting."

"We can't let her turn away now," Ace snarled.

"We won't." Major glanced at them over his shoulder. "She's ours."

"About fucking time," Rocco muttered. "How do we—"

"We come in for breakfast, lunch, and dinner. We ask her out every time we're here until she says yes," Major stated emphatically.

"And if she doesn't say yes?" Ace asked.

"She will."

"I hope you're fucking right." Rocco scrubbed his hand over his face and sighed.

Delta exited the office without looking back. Major led the way down the hall. Rocco was pleased to see their woman sitting in a booth with Cindy and Enya as she ate a sandwich, and figured Lilac was in the kitchen prepping food for the next day.

He kept his gaze on her as Major tugged the door open and stepped over the threshold. Rocco felt an itch at his nape and glanced up and down the street, but he didn't see anything or anyone suspicious. When he gazed back over his shoulder toward Delta and she quickly ducked her head as if she hadn't been watching them, he smiled.

She was more interested in them than she was letting on.

It was time to head home and make some plans.

Rocco and his brothers were on a mission and they weren't giving up until they had their woman right where they wanted her.

Chapter Seven

Delta gasped and bolted upright in bed. Every night she fell into bed exhausted and just before she sank into sleep she prayed this would be the night she didn't have the nightmare. Sometimes it came almost as soon as she fell asleep, and other times not till she was about to wake up. She relived that horrifying moment of being shot over and over, and while sometimes she felt as if she was going crazy, she knew she wasn't. She'd knew she had a form of PTSD, and while the panic attacks had lessened, sometimes they took hold when she least expected it.

She glanced over at her digital bedside clock and frowned when she didn't see the glowing red numbers illuminating in the darkness. She reached under her pillow, grabbed her cell phone and activated the screen. It was just after three in the morning. Knowing from experience she wouldn't go back to sleep right away, she flung the covers aside and headed to the bathroom. After using the facilities, washing her hands and wiping the sweat from her face with a damp cloth, she headed toward the small kitchen. She was thirsty and needed a drink.

She'd just opened the fridge and removed the jug of water when she felt a vibration under her feet. Frowning, she placed the full jug on the counter and headed for the stairs. She flicked the light switch at the top of the staircase and shivered when no light came on. Had there been a storm? Was the power out? How long had the power been out? It could have been minutes or hours. There was no way for her to tell.

Delta gripped her cell phone so tight it bit into her fingers as she crept down the stairs to the locked door. She placed her hand on the door and held her breath. She nearly screamed with fright when something, or someone, bashed on the door. She turned and fled back up the stairs, swiping a finger over her now dark cell phone screen and brought up the number pad. She was about to call 9-1-1 but the dispatcher would likely think she was a prank call since she couldn't speak.

Too scared to remain alone. It took a few moments to remember that she'd saved Major's, Rocco's and Ace's cell numbers into her phone. Thank God, Major had written them down and she'd had the foresight to keep them. Ace's number was first on the list and after bringing it up she began texting, all the while hoping his phone wasn't on do not disturb, silent, or off.

Was there a storm? The power's out and I think someone's broken into the diner. Can you please call the sheriffs for me? Delta.

She stared at the door and covered her mouth with her hand when it shook. Whoever was out there didn't look as if they were going to give up. She was shaking so much she wasn't sure how she was still standing, but she couldn't give into her fear and end up hysterical. After inhaling a deep breath through her nose and exhaling in calm measured breaths, her brain started working again. Delta moved back up the stairs to her apartment backward, her gaze still locked to the door, thanking whichever god was listening that the deadbolt to the stairwell door seemed to be strong. Just as her foot connected with the top step, the door shuddered again. Her eyes widened with horror when she noticed the doorframe was beginning to splinter.

She spun around so quickly she lost her balance and ended up landing on her hands and knees, both her shins slamming into the edge of the top step. She bit down hard on her lip so she wouldn't cry out in pain and shoved back to her feet. When she'd fallen, her phone had skittered out of her hand and since the screen was dark, and the casing was black she couldn't see it. When she felt a vibration under her bare feet she knew she'd run out of time. Delta raced through the living room, back into her bedroom, closing the door behind her. The lock on the bedroom door was flimsy but it might be enough to slow whoever was after her down, so she flipped it. She hurried to the adjoining bathroom, closed and locked that door, too.

She switched the light on and cursed when it didn't work, but she moved farther into the room and began to rummage around in the cupboard looking for a weapon. There was nothing. Delta didn't even have a pair of nail scissors since she kept her nails clipped short. There was no hair spray or even a larger pair of scissors. Mentally cursing herself for not taking the time to go and shop for a first aid kit like she'd planned, she pulled the towels and face cloths out and threw them into the tub. The only thing left was some toothpaste, a new toothbrush, a small tub of vitamin E cream, and a can of deodorant.

Grabbing the can of deodorant and hoping like hell she wouldn't have to use it, since that would mean she would be way too close to whoever had broken in, she moved back to the door and sat with her back against it. Tears of fear and panic burned her eyes but she wasn't about to let them fall. She needed to keep her emotions under control, keep herself together in case she had to fight. And fight she would. This time she wasn't going to just stand there in shock and let someone shoot her again. She would fight with everything she had, even if she ended up dying.

* * * *

Ace felt as if he'd just fallen asleep when he heard his phone vibrate, and since he never got texts or calls in the middle of the night, he knew something was wrong. He turned his beside lamp on, grasped his phone, swiped his thumb over the screen and opened the message. His heart flipped in his chest and anger raced through his blood. He was on his feet before he even realized he'd moved.

"Major! Rocco! Get dressed. Now!" Ace shouted.

"What the fuck!" Rocco snarled.

Ace ignored his brother's surliness as he grabbed his clothes, pulling them on quickly. He texted Delta back hoping she would heed him and didn't try and take on whoever had broken into the diner by herself. *Go into your bedroom and lock the door. Don't open it for anyone. We'll be there as fast as we can.*

"What's going on?" Major asked as he entered Ace's bedroom, tugging his T-shirt over his head.

Ace held up his finger as he made a call. "Luke, someone's just broken into the diner. Can you send someone over?"

"Okay, thanks. Yeah we're on our way." Ace was already on the move and didn't need to look back to know that his brothers had heard his call and were following him.

Since they worked on the land and encountered snakes and other dangerous animals from time to time, he and his brothers always carried their registered guns. Usually they didn't take them with them when they went to town, but this situation wasn't usual. Ace was glad, too, that his brothers were packing their pistols just like he was.

Major, Rocco, and Ace jumped into the truck and Major took off before Ace had even closed his door. He disconnected the call and tugged his seatbelt on.

"Talk!" Major ordered.

"I got a text from Delta asking if there'd been a storm since her power was out. Then she said she thought someone had broken into the diner."

"Fuck! Faster, Major."

Major didn't respond, but pressed his foot down harder on the gas. Ace clung to the handle above the door and held his breath as his brother drifted the truck around a ninety-degree turn. Thank fuck they'd all had advanced driving training while they were in the Marines.

"Did you text her back?" Rocco asked angrily.

Ace knew that anger wasn't directed at him. "Yeah. I told her to lock herself in the bedroom and not open the door for anyone."

"Why the fuck didn't the Alcott guys call us? They should have realized something wasn't right," Rocco snarled.

Since Ace didn't have an answer, he didn't respond. He wasn't a security expert, but with a power outage, he suspected that all alarms and cameras would be out of action.

Ace nearly sighed in relief when he saw the flashing blue and red lights of the sheriff's vehicle outside the diner, but when he saw the damage done to the building, he was the one seeing red. Rage like he'd never felt before left a haze over his eyes and he was actually shaking. Every single window of the diner had been smashed. Tables had been ripped away from walls and out of the bolts on the floors. The linoleum floor had been slashed as had the cushioned booth seats. The display cabinet had been tipped over and that was just the damage he could see.

God only knew what had been done to the rest of the place.

* * * *

Major was out of the car and running toward Luke and Damon who were standing amongst the destruction. "Where's Delta? Is she all right? Who the fuck did this? Did you catch the fucker?"

"Whoever it was is long gone," Luke answered. The muscles in his jaw were ticking and Major knew he was just as pissed as he was.

"We're hoping Delta is upstairs in her room. The door is closed and locked but there's no way for us to get in there without busting it down. We don't want to scare her more than she has to be already."

"This is personal," Damon said. "This wasn't just a random act. Whoever did this wants Delta to suffer."

"Why?" Rocco snapped as he moved to stand next to Major.

Ace moved to his other side. Major was glad for his brother's support. There was no fucking way they were letting Luke and Damon hedge any longer. Delta was in danger and the only way he and his brothers could keep her safe was if they knew the full story.

"I don't know about this," Luke began. "As far as I know she doesn't have any enemies."

"Well, you're obviously wrong." Ace glanced around at the debris. "What aren't you telling us?"

"Delta moved here from Chicago," Damon said.

Luke scrubbed a hand down his face. "She used to work at a bank and was shot during a bad hold up."

"Geezus. Mother fucking son of a bitch." Major spun around, intending to pace, but there wasn't a clear path. Instead, he drew his foot back and kicked at an upturned chair, sending it flying. The pain in his foot was minimal since he wore steel-capped cowboy boots, a necessity when working with animals. He had to concentrate on controlling his breathing to get his fury under wraps.

"That's why she hides away and has a hard time trusting," Rocco stated.

Damon nodded.

"The fucker who shot her." Ace clenched his fists. "What happened to him?"

"He died," Luke answered. "The security guard shot him."

"Thank fuck for that," Major said in a growly voice. "This can't be for revenge."

"We can't be certain of that," Damon said. "The asshole could have had an accomplice that no one knew about."

"Was the security footage reviewed?" Rocco asked.

"With a fine toothed-comb."

"So we're back at square fucking one and have no idea who, or why someone is out to get our woman?"

"That's the size of it," Luke answered. "I'm sorry, guys. I wish I had the answers but I don't. What I do know is that Delta is in danger. It's no longer safe for her to be here on her own."

"You're right." Major nodded. "I just hope she agrees with us."

"How are we going to get her out of her room without scaring the shit out of her?" Damon asked.

Ace held up his cell phone. "Leave that to me."

* * * *

Delta had no idea how much time had passed and though it seemed to pass quickly, it also felt as if hours had gone by. She knew that was because of the adrenaline surging through her blood, and while she tried to keep her fear at bay, she was struggling. Her emotions were warring from anger to fear and back again. She was cold since she was only wearing the usual boy shorts and tank she always slept it, but she was also coated with a fine sheen of perspiration.

Her hands were trembling and the knuckles on her right hand were aching from holding the can of deodorant for so long and so tightly. She wasn't sure she'd be able to uncurl her fingers and let the can go. There hadn't been any vibrations for a while now, and though she wanted to open the door to find out if whoever had been trying to break in was still there, or had left, she was too scared to.

A sob caught in her throat and she swallowed it back down as she wished she still had her cell phone with her. She had no idea if Ace had received her text or not. Had he called the sheriffs? What if he was still sound asleep and totally oblivious to her predicament.

She glanced down at her hand when something plopped onto her skin and blinked the blurriness from her eyes. She was crying and hadn't even noticed that she was.

When she felt the floor vibrate again, the trembling in her limbs and body grew worse. She covered her mouth with her free hand and tried not to inhale too deeply through her nose. The vibration stopped and she canted her head as if she was trying to listen for noise, but in actual fact she was honing into all four of her other senses. Luckily, her eyes had adjusted to the lack of light a while ago.

The moon was bright in the night sky and some of the bathroom was illuminated because of the midsized window above the vanity mirror. At least she wasn't totally in the dark, but since the power was out, she wasn't about to leave her safe sanctuary. If the person was still out there, they could use the dark to hide in the shadows.

She might not be the most intelligent person in the world, but she definitely wasn't stupid.

When a thud vibrated down her back she knew her time had run out. She rolled onto her hands and knees, tucking the can of spray under her chin, and crawled away from the door. The only semi-safe place was in the bathtub. Hopefully, if this guy started shooting the tub would protect her from getting shot.

It took her three tries to ease her body over the rim of the bath since she was shaking so much. She pushed herself to the far end, grasped the can in her hand and held it up ready.

When the door burst open she drew in a deep breath and screamed as loud and as long as she could, hoping that someone would hear her and call the sheriffs. A tall, broad silhouette of a man loomed in the now open entry and Delta screamed again. The beam of a flashlight bounced over the floor, but instead of pointing in her direction the beam turned toward the hulking brute in the bathroom doorway.

The can dropped from her shaking hand onto the floor and rolled away. Delta covered her face and sobbed with relief.

She was safe. Ace had gotten her text after all.

* * * *

Ace had never been so relieved to hear a woman scream in his life. His ears hurt from the volume of Delta's loud terror but he didn't care. All he cared about was that she was safe, unharmed.

He hated that he'd had to break the door down and frighten her but there was no way in hell he was leaving her locked in that bathroom all alone, in case she'd been hurt. His first instinct had been to shine his flashlight in her direction but that would have frightened her even more. Thankfully, his Marine skills would never be lost and he'd shone that beam of light onto his own face so she could see who he was.

Ace was at her side in seconds. He dropped the flashlight onto the floor, and grasped her upper arms and lifted her out of the tub. She wrapped her arms so tightly around his neck she was almost strangling him, but again, he didn't give a shit. She was safe in his arms where she belonged, and if he had anything to say about it, she was never leaving.

He sank down onto the floor on his ass and wrapped his arms around her slim body, holding and rocking her as she cried her heart out. Her sobs wracked her whole body and while he hated hearing her cry, he knew she needed to get rid of the fear and adrenaline coursing through her blood.

Major and Rocco knelt on the floor on either side of them, which was a tight fit in such a small room, but Ace knew they needed to touch her, to feel her warmth against theirs, to know she was safe just as much as he did. Finally, her sobs died down until the occasional hiccup jerked her body and she drew in deep ragged breaths.

Ace continued to caress a hand up and down her back as he nudged her chin up. The room was brighter with three powerful flashlights in the room and he had no trouble seeing her eyes. They were streaked with red and puffy from her crying, but she was still so fucking beautiful.

He and Rocco had been taking sign language lessons from Major, and while he wasn't very proficient he was learning and knew enough to get by, but right now, there was no way he was removing the arm he had wrapped around her waist. "Are you okay, darlin'? Are you hurt?"

Delta shook her head and then rested it against his chest.

"Let me take her," Major said, and though Ace didn't want to relinquish her, he needed to get them up off the floor.

Ace nodded, gripped her hips as Major clasped her arms, and they helped her up. When she swayed on her feet, Rocco moved in behind her and hooked an arm around her waist while he and Major rose.

Delta looked up at Rocco over her shoulder, turned in his arms and wrapped her arms around his waist. Ace caressed a hand over her head, hair, and down her back, needing constant contact for reassurance. Reassurance that she was fine other than being scared out of her mind.

Rocco lifted her into his arms and Delta wrapped her arms around his neck and her legs around his waist. "I'm taking her to the truck."

Ace and Major followed her out into her bedroom. Ace turned toward her closet and dresser, and after rummaging around for a bag, began packing her some clothes. Major was in the small living room talking with Luke and Damon, but he could hear them easily.

"You taking her back to your place?" Luke asked.

"Yes."

"We'll come by first thing to get her statement. Get her settled for the rest of the night. We're going to be here for a while dusting for prints and taking photos of the damage," Luke explained.

"Do you know if she's insured?" Damon asked.

"I hope so, but if it won't matter if she's not. We've got more than enough money to help fix the place up," Major stated. "Have either of you been able to contact the Alcott men?"

"Not yet, but we're working on it."

Ace entered the living room to see Damon running his fingers through his hair. "This would never have happened if Giles, Remy, or Brandon had been monitoring things. They took a trip out of town and decided to stay overnight to give Kayli a night off. Britt, Dan, and Debbie Delaney were looking after their kids for the night."

"So who the fuck was watching the monitors?" Major asked.

"A newbie they trained. The Alcotts are going to be devastated when they find out what went down. The new guy will probably get the axe."

"They should never have left the new guy on their own if he didn't know what he was doing." Ace glared at Luke and Damon before he sucked in a deep, calming breath and released it. He shouldn't be taking his anger out on the sheriffs and his friends since none of this was their fault. "Sorry."

"Don't worry, we know what you're going through. Every man in this town is going to be as angry as you are. If I know the Alcotts, and I like to believe I do, they'll make a claim on their insurance and foot the bill for the refurbishment of the diner," Damon said.

"We'll see." Major frowned.

Luke clapped Ace and then Major on the shoulder. "Go take your woman home. We'll see you in the morning."

Ace shook both men's hands and headed out. He couldn't wait to have Delta in their home, needing to know she would be safe while under their protection. He and his brothers weren't about to let her out of their sight again, no matter how hard she argued.

When they got her settled, he, Major, and Rocco would need to sit down and talk things over. Even though he knew Delta was going to kick up a stink, one of them would be with her at all times. They'd take turns being with her so they knew she was safe.

Chapter Eight

Rocco got into the back seat of the truck, taking Delta with him. He was glad she didn't protest. When he was settled with her in his lap, he grabbed the jacket Major had left on the back seat and draped it over her. Anger surged anew when he caught sight of the puckered scar where a bullet had pierced her shoulder, and the thin surgical line where a doctor had cut her open to get the bullet out. He wanted to ask her about the injury but now wasn't the time. It had taken a long time for her to stop trembling, and now that she was resting quietly in his arms, he didn't want to disturb her, even though he knew she wasn't asleep.

She was so fucking small compared to him and his brothers. Delta was curled up on his lap with her knees bent up and her cheek pressed against his chest. Every now and then she'd shiver and tremble, but for the most part she was calm. Ace breathed in her warm, feminine scent, content to hold her for as long as she let him, and hoped she didn't kick up a stink when they took her home with them.

Major and Ace walked toward the truck and Rocco was pleased to see that Ace had packed at bag for Delta. When his brothers opened the front doors and got into the truck, she didn't move. Rocco began to think she'd fallen asleep after all, but when Ace turned to gaze at her, then smiled and winked he knew she hadn't.

Maybe she was too exhausted to worry about anything right now. She'd been through a terrifying ordeal and was no doubt sapped of energy. Add in the fact she'd been working crazy long hours with only one wait person to help her out, Rocco wondered how the hell she'd kept going for as long as she had. Maybe the destruction of her diner was a blessing in disguise so she could have some much needed rest. He mentally shook his head. No, he'd rather that she'd been able to take time off to have a break than it being forced on her in such a terrifying way.

Rocco kissed the top of her head and sighed with contentment when she nuzzled his chest with her cheek. He met Major's gaze as his brother turned to back the truck out of the parking lot. Major had a new light in his eyes that Rocco had never seen before, and he knew it was all because of the woman in his arms. There was a lightness that hadn't been there before they'd joined the military.

He and his brothers had seen so much violence and death, they'd had to close themselves off and become the hard, emotionless men they were today to deal with such things. Sometimes, Rocco thought he'd never be able to feel, to open his heart to a woman let alone recognize the one when she came into his and his brothers' lives, but that hadn't been the case. He was so fucking glad about that, and while he wanted to move this attraction they had for each other forward, he was going to wait and see how things went.

From what Luke and Damon had said, Delta had also had a lot of shit to deal with and they would need to go at her pace so they didn't send her running. He hoped she didn't have PTSD, but figured after what she'd been through, she probably did. And then he knew for a fact she did when be remembered how she'd gotten dizzy as she hyperventilated the night they'd first met her. He and his brothers had also had to deal with the after effects of fighting a war, but working on the land had helped ease the consequences. At least they would be able to help her if she had nightmares and flashbacks. They'd been through it all themselves.

Rocco knew the moment she drifted off to sleep. Her body got heavier as her muscles relaxed and that made him feel ecstatic. She might not realize it yet, but Delta trusted him and his brothers. He only hoped she trusted them enough to hang around and be in a relationship with them.

"How is she?" Major asked as he turned into their driveway.

"Asleep."

"That's good." Ace turned to meet his gaze before looking at Delta. There was a softness in his younger brother's eyes Rocco had never seen before and he suspected he probably looked the same, but he didn't care. He just wanted to savor having her in his arms for as long as he could.

Major parked the truck close to the verandah steps, turned off the ignition, and got out. Ace was already hurrying to the front door to unlock it. Major opened the rear passenger door as Rocco gently and carefully lifted Delta into his arms. He didn't want to wake her now that she was sleeping. There were still dark smudges under her eyes, and he knew she been working crazy hours trying to keep the diner up and running.

"Let me take her," Major said

Rocco shifted to plant one foot on the ground and carefully maneuvered Delta out the door as he stood up. "I've got her."

Major nodded and ran his fingers through his hair but didn't say anything. Rocco knew he wanted to hold her as much as he did, but he was going to keep her where she was until he got her inside. It would only be a minute or so before he had to put her down. Never had a woman felt so right in his arms. Her slight weight was perfect as was her womanly scent. Everything about Delta Sykes was absolutely perfect, and he was determined to have her in his life for the rest of his. Rocco just hoped she would agree to be with him and his brothers, because he wasn't sure what he'd do if she didn't.

* * * *

Major was more than a little envious of Rocco having the chance to hold Delta for so long, but he pushed his jealousy aside. This wasn't about him or his brothers. This was about Delta and her needs. They needed to find out what the hell was going on, why someone had targeted the diner and essentially their woman. He was so damn angry at whoever had scared Delta, but until they found the culprit there was nothing to be done.

Ace had gone ahead of him and Rocco, straight to the recently renovated master bedroom they'd set up in the hope of finding the one woman that was perfect for him and his brothers to share. Major just nodded his affirmation when Ace met his gaze and his brothers smiled and nodded back before tugging the covers back.

Rocco carefully eased Delta onto the mattress on her side, and after removing the jacket he'd used to cover her gorgeous body with, he and Ace pulled the quilt up over her. He nodded toward the doorway, indicating his brothers to follow him out.

Ace followed him, but when he didn't hear Rocco move he paused in the doorway and glanced back. His brother was thinking better than he, for which he was glad. Rocco had turned the bedside lamp off, but flicked the light on in the adjacent bathroom on before closing the door almost all the way, so Delta could find her way about if she woke up and needed the facilities.

Major hurried down the hall and snagged three beers from the fridge, and handed them to his brothers before taking the cap off and taking a slug.

"I hate that no one knows who has it in for Delta." Ace sipped at his beer.

Just as Major was about to agree, his cell phone rang. He pulled it from his pocket and frowned when he saw he didn't know who was calling but answered anyway, putting it on speaker so his brothers could hear.

"Hello?"

"Major Porter?"

"Who's asking?"

"This is Giles Alcott."

"And?" Major couldn't quite keep the bite of anger from his voice.

"I called to apologize to you, your brothers, and Delta. We had a new guy monitoring things and we thought he was up to speed, enough to leave him on his own for the night. Obviously, I was wrong."

Major was too angry to go easy on the security expert. "Obviously."

"My brothers and I are going to foot the bill to fix the diner and replace any stock that was lost or damaged. I assure you something like this will never, *ever* happen again."

"You'd better make sure it doesn't. If Delta hadn't been able to contact us—I don't even want to think about what could have happened to her."

"Yeah, I know. I am so damn sorry. We've never had anything like this happen before, and I can tell you now, it'll never fucking happen again."

"Okay," Major replied. "Thanks for the call and for footing the damage bill. I'll let Delta know when she wakes up."

"How'd you know she was with us?" Rocco frowned suspiciously.

"Luke Sun-Walker."

"That explains it," Ace said.

"Yeah, he called me after he and Damon secured the diner to let me know what had happened. He was just as angry as you three are, and rightly so. The guy monitoring the system should have picked up that something was going on. He's had more than adequate training. You might be happy to know we've fired his ass."

"Will that come back on us?" Major asked, worriedly.

"No, we'll make sure of it."

"Okay, thanks for the call Giles."

"Sure. We'll have contractors start work first thing. Remy, Brandon, and I would like to meet with Delta to apologize."

"I'll let you know," Major replied.

"Fair enough." Giles sighed. "See you soon."

"Yeah." Major ended the call.

"That was nice of him," Ace said. "He didn't have to do that."

"No, but something like this should never have happened in the first place."

"Don't go holding a grudge on the Alcotts, Major." Ace threaded his fingers through his hair. "Giles feels bad enough as is, and he's trying to make amends."

"I know." Major gulped the rest of his beer before tossing the bottle into the recycling. "She could have been fucking hurt."

"Thankfully, she wasn't." Rocco pointed out.

"Yeah, yeah." Major sighed as he turned toward the doorway. "I'm going to get a couple hours of sleep. I suggest you two do the same."

He paused outside his bedroom door, gazing at the nearly closed master bedroom door until he heard his brothers' footsteps. With a sigh of resignation, he entered his room and started to undress. He had a feeling he wasn't going to get any sleep at all.

* * * *

Delta's heart flipped and then slammed painfully against her ribs when she saw the small white toy gun aimed at her. Her lips twitched with humor, but when she met the guy's eyes, fear came roaring back. She knew she'd been here before, and while she tried to force herself out of the nightmare, she couldn't. It was the same nearly every night, and things would play out until she woke up gasping for breath. Even though she didn't hear the pistol fire, she watched the stream of smoke wafting from the tip and then agony slammed into her shoulder. She screamed and screamed trying to alert the security guard, the other employees, and the customers to what was going on.

The man turned away from her and just as she took another breath to scream again, he stumbled and went down to the floor. Dark red blood began pooling under him, and while she tried to make herself look away from the gruesome macabre scene, she couldn't. Her vision got blurry and although she tried to lock her knees, they buckled. She hit the floor with a grunt, her mouth open in a silent scream as agony shot through her shoulder, down her arm, up her neck, and into her head.

Hands reached for her, lifting her from the floor and she jolted awake.

It took her few moments to realize that the last part hadn't been part of her dream. She was sitting in Major's lap and he was rocking her back and forth as if she were a child. The tears she tried to keep at bay welled and spilled over her lids before rolling down her cheeks. Her whole body shuddered as the first sob surged up from her chest and out of her mouth. She wrapped her arms around Major's waist and clung to him while the storm raged, until finally her tears slowed and then ceased.

She tensed when she felt another hand caressing up and down her back, and yet another up and down her arm. Major wasn't alone. Ace and Rocco were with him.

Delta figured she must have been screaming in her sleep and woken the men up. She felt a little guilty over that, but there was nothing she could do about it. After removing her arms from around Major's waist, she wiped her cheeks with the back of her hands and sniffed.

Tissues were shoved into one of her hands and she blew her nose before lifting her gaze to Major's. He was looking down but he wasn't looking into her eyes. When she followed his train of sight, she gasped and tugged at the tank top. The strap had fallen off her shoulder, and the ugly round bullet wound and surgical scar were clearly visible.

Major nudged her gaze back up to his.

"Did you have a nightmare, baby?"

She nodded and then apologized. "I'm sorry for waking you all."

Rocco shifted closer to her side and that was when she realized that all three men were nearly naked. Heat suffused her cheeks and while she tried to keep her gaze from wandering, it was impossible. She licked her lips as she took in Rocco's broad muscular shoulders, toned pecs, and defined abs. The man was built and his skin was bronzed with a healthy tan. All three of the Porter men were the epitome of every woman's wet dream, and the more she looked, the stronger the urge to touch got.

She turned her gaze to her other side when a finger stroked down her arm eliciting a shiver to race up her spine and goosebumps to spread over her skin.

Ace was taller than Rocco by about an inch, and he was more muscular than his brother, but not in that horrible body builder kind of way. He was built more like a linebacker, and boy was he handsome. All the Porter men were divine to look at. She could have stared at them all day long. The hue of Ace's gray eyes seemed to change with his moods and right now, they looked as if they were blazing with fire. At first she thought he was angry with her for waking him up, but quickly discarded that thought when his gaze wandered up and down her body as he licked his lips. When he lifted his gaze to hers once more, there was so much heat in his eyes there was no mistaking the lust.

When she shifted in Major's lap and felt something hard poking into her ass and thigh, she froze. She lowered her gaze as she tried to get the arousal simmering in her blood under control, but she made the mistake of staring at his wide chest. His pectorals jumped and twitched when he moved his arms and she couldn't help but let her eyes wander, yet again. There was hair on his chest between his pecs and she wondered if it was as soft as it looked. Delta didn't even realize she was moving until her hand landed on his warm skin. She licked her lips and sighed when his soft chest hairs tickled her fingers. She shifted her gaze to the small bronzed colored nipples and watched with fascination as they hardened. She hadn't known a man's nipples could do the same as a woman's, but now that she did, she wondered if he'd like to have those nipples licked and sucked.

She gasped when her breasts swelled and her nipples hardened, and had to bite her lip when her pussy moistened and clenched. That wasn't the only response to being so close to these three sexy, nearly naked men. Her clit was throbbing as if it had its own heartbeat, and she was aching so much she wanted to shove her hand down her boy shorts and rub her engorged nub.

It didn't seem to matter to her body that she'd only known these three men for a very short time. It took everything she had to keep her attraction to them hidden, but right now she had no idea why that had been so important. She craved to have them kissing and touching her. She craved to have their arms around her and holding her. She craved to have them love her.

But most of all, she craved for them to take the deep-seated liquid ache away.

Chapter Nine

Delta couldn't seem to catch her breath and while she tried to pull her gaze away from all that delectable naked skin, she couldn't. That was until Major nudged her eyes up to his. The moment she met his fiery, gray-blue gaze, she knew she was lost.

She could have pulled away or lowered her eyes when she saw he was leaning closer and closer to her, but she did neither of those things. Instead, she licked her lips and then closed her lids. He brushed his lips back and forth over hers as if testing her response, and when he opened his mouth over hers, she was a goner. All thought fled from her mind as his tongue invaded her mouth. She didn't consciously think about wrapping her arms around his neck, or leaning in closer to him, but knew she had when her fingers brushed against his silky-soft, cool, sandy-brown hair. Her aching breasts pressed against his naked chest and she moaned as her nipples tightened even more.

Major caressed his hand up her back, his fingers threading into her hair and he cupped the back of her head. And then he was devouring her. His tongue delved deep before coming back to slide along and then twirl around hers. Delta whimpered as she angled her head a little more to the side as she kissed him back rapaciously.

She'd thought her body had been on fire before, but that was nothing compared to the way she was burning up on the inside now. She was so hungry for more, she wanted to pull away from him, strip the clothes from her body and beg for his touch over every inch of her body.

When he broke the kiss, she had to swallow her groan of disappointed frustration so she didn't look too needy, and while the urge to open her eyes to meet his gaze was strong, she ignored it. Or tried to until he tugged gently on her hair to get her attention.

She drew in a deep, steady breath and hoped her breathing would even out quickly, but suspected it wouldn't when there was so much delicious manly flesh on display. She opened her eyes when Major clasped her waist and lifted her to sit on the mattress beside him.

She met his gaze when he stroked a finger down her face and then lowered her eyes to his fingers as he signed to her.

"We all want you, baby," Major said. "We all want to make love with you, have a relationship with you."

Delta wanted the same, and though she knew it was going to be hard to find time to spend with them with her obligations to the diner, she wanted to say yes. She'd never been attracted to any other man, and while being attracted to three men was more than a little nerve wracking, she didn't want to walk away. She wanted to know what it was like to make love, to be held and to be needed, but if she gave in and gave them what they wanted—her body—would they walk away from her afterward?

She turned her gaze toward Rocco when he tapped her on the thigh.

"What has you hesitating, honey?" Rocco signed, haltingly.

Tears of gratitude burned the back of her eyes that he would take time out of his busy life to learn sign language just so he could communicate with her.

Ace caressed a hand down her arm to gain her attention and then he signed as he spoke. "What's wrong, darlin'? Talk to us. Tell us, what's going through your mind?"

"Why me?"

"Why you what?" Major asked.

"What's so special about me? You guys are all very handsome. You could have your pick of any woman you wanted."

"We don't want just any woman, Delta," Major said. "We want you."

"But why?"

"You have no idea how gorgeously sexy you are, do you?"

She shook her head. She didn't think she was ugly, but she didn't think she was gorgeous or sexy, either.

Major continued. "You are such a strong person and you've got a big heart, although you try to hide it. Did you think we didn't notice the hurt in your eyes when you told us you couldn't get anyone to work under you? Do you think we don't see the sadness in your soul you try to hide, or the yearning looks whenever you gaze at us?"

"I don't—"

"Don't." Rocco slashed his hand in the air. "Don't you deny the attraction between us, honey. We've been around the block a time or two and know when a woman is attracted to us."

"So what?" Delta signed. "I'll bet if you walk down the street you'd see a myriad of woman ogling your attributes."

"We don't care about any other women," Ace said. "We only care about you."

"What makes me so special? And if I did agree to have…sex with you, what then?"

"What do you mean what then?" Major asked.

"Will you turn your backs after you've gotten what you wanted?"

Major stared deeply into her eyes and frowned. "Who hurt you, Delta?"

"No one hurt me," she replied.

He lowered his gaze to her shoulder before locking eyes with her again. "That was a lie, which we'll come back to, but I want to know who made you scared of relationships."

"I'm not scared of relationships," she signed rapidly. "How could I be when I've never had one before."

"And why is that?" Major asked.

She gnawed on her lip and shook her head.

"What are you so afraid of, baby?"

The emotion in his eyes had her heart flipping in her chest. Major looked as if he genuinely cared for her, but how could that be when he'd only known her for a few days?

Rocco caressed her bare thigh, causing her to shiver. "Where do you parents live, Delta?"

She didn't want to answer, but from the implacable resolve in Rocco's gaze, he wasn't going anywhere until she did. When she glanced at Ace and Major she noticed they were both watching her avidly, too.

"I don't have any parents." Her heart was beating a rapid staccato inside her chest and she was panting. Tears of humiliation and dejection burned her eyes, but she didn't let them fall. She'd done more than enough crying and wasn't about to fall apart in front of these three, strong, confident men again. Delta had learned a long time ago that tears never solved anything, even if the release of emotions was sometimes cathartic.

"Where did you grow up?" Major asked.

"In an institution for the deaf and blind." She couldn't believe she was answering them. Normally she never talked about herself, but there was something about Major, Rocco, and Ace that set her at ease, which was a direct contradiction to the way her stomach was roiling.

"Was it a good place?" Ace asked.

She met each of their gazes, and when she noticed none of them were watching her with pity she relaxed a little more. "It wasn't bad. I learned how to take care of myself, how to sign, and got a good education."

"Yet you keep yourself apart from others," Rocco said. "Why?"

"Why do you think?" she replied. "Do you know what it's like to be treated differently because of a disability? All through my life I've been shunned because I'm deaf. I was even kept apart from the other employees when I worked at the bank in Chicago. The manger had a teller window set up across the other side of the room, away from everyone else. Do you know what it's like to be singled out day after day just because you're different to everyone else? If the manager hadn't done that, maybe I wouldn't have been targeted and shot in the bank hold up.

"No one wants to be around someone who can't hear them. No one wants to have a relationship with a deaf person."

"You're wrong, Delta. Maybe not about other people, but about us you are. You don't like to be pigeon holed any more than we do. Don't judge us by the action of others. We aren't out to hurt you, baby," Major said. "We don't just want to have sex with you. We want to make love with you, and have a relationship with you."

"Major's right," Ace signed. "If we just wanted sex we could go and pick up a woman without any difficulty. We think you're special. We think we could have a long-lasting relationship with you, but we won't know unless we all try."

Rocco cupped her face in his hand. "We want everything with you, honey. We want the picket fence, the two point five kids. We want to spend years fighting and loving with you. Don't you want that, too?"

The yearning in her heart was so strong, she couldn't help but nod. She lowered her eyes and then looked up to meet each of their gazes again. "What if we start something and you find out I'm not the person you think I am?"

"That won't happen, baby," Major said. "We know our own minds, our own hearts. We aren't young kids just starting out to explore life. We've all spent ten or more years serving our country, and when we were on leave, we partied hard. We've had more women between us and singularly than I want to admit, but not one single one of those women ever got to me the way you do. You're it for us, Delta, and if you'd just give us a chance we want to be it for you, too."

She licked her dry lips and thought about how she'd feel if she turned her back on them and was surprised by the pain that shot straight into her heart. How could she feel so much for three men she barely knew? But more importantly, how could she walk away?

If she denied them, would she be left with regrets? The answer to that question was a resounding hell yes. She'd always dreamed of being loved for who she was, disability and all. These three men were offering all her dreams to her on a platter. She'd be a fool to reject them.

She might very well be a virgin, but she wasn't naïve. She used to read all the time and her favorite genre was romance no matter what the sub-genre was. She'd read historical, paranormal, suspense and contemporary romance books, but her favorite was erotic romance. She wanted that happily ever after she'd read about. She wanted to experience passion and love. She wanted to be held, but most of all she wanted to be accepted, warts and all.

Major, Rocco, and Ace had already proven by their actions they were good honorable men. They'd stepped in and helped her time and again. Most importantly of all, they treated her like a normal human being. They didn't talk down to her, or look at her as if she was an anomaly just because she was deaf.

Add in the explosive attraction that seemed to be simmering between them and her, she'd be an idiot to deny them, and herself.

It was scary to put herself out there to be hurt, but she was absolutely terrified at the thought of being alone for the rest of her life. Not because she wasn't independent and couldn't look after herself, but because of the endless loneliness. She'd spent her whole life on the outside looking in.

Until she'd set up shop in Slick Rock and seen all the other polyandrous relationships, she hadn't realized just how very lonely she really was. Delta knew it wouldn't matter if she was surrounded by people. She would still feel that deep, dark emptiness that resided inside of her heart and soul.

She didn't want to turn away. She didn't want to live the rest of her life in silent solitude. This was her chance at liberation. Her chance to be treated normal and live just like any other person. She could throw off the virtual shackles placed around her by society and grab hold of what was on offer.

"I…yes."

"What?" All three men asked at the same time.

"Yes what, baby?" Major slid from the side of the bed to his knees before he turned to face her.

She couldn't believe how tall he was. Even with him down on his knees his gaze was almost level with hers. She licked her suddenly dry lips and nodded.

"You need to spell it out for us, Delta." Major's hands landed on her bare knees and then caressed up and down her thighs. When he nudged her legs apart so he could insinuate himself between them, her breath caught in her throat and the smoldering fire simmering in her blood started to get hotter. Her breasts were achy, her nipples hardened and her clit pulsed. Each time he smoothed his hands over her bare skin she mentally pleaded him to go higher. Her need for him, Rocco, and Ace was so intense she wasn't sure how much longer she could endure it without getting any relief.

She closed her eyes to give herself a second or two to get her thoughts together, and when she opened them she met each of the men's gazes before signing her answer as succinctly as possible.

"Yes, I want to make love with you, to try a relationship with you all."

They exploded into motion.

She gasped when Rocco grasped her hips, lifted her and shifted toward the edge of the bed before placing her in his lap with her back to him, her legs draping over the outside of his.

Major moved back between her splayed thighs and just as she reached for him, her wrists were shackled in Rocco's hands. She turned to glance at him but didn't get the chance to meet his gaze.

Ace moved closer to her side, cupped her cheek in his large, warm, callused hand and turned her eyes toward him. She'd no sooner blinked and inhaled when his mouth was on hers.

Delta moaned as she opened to him, allowing him entrance to her mouth, and she wasn't disappointed. His tongue licked into her mouth to dance and duel with hers until she was panting.

She groaned when Rocco released her wrists and whimpered when he caressed his hands up her sides toward the outside of her breasts. She arched toward him, begging him without words to touch her, to relieve the incessant ache she'd had since the very first night she'd set her gaze on them. Her cry of delight vibrated in her chest and was probably muffled by Ace's mouth when Rocco gave her what she wanted, what she craved.

His hands enveloped her breasts through the thin cotton of the tank top and he kneaded and molded her feminine globes. And it was an amazing sensation but not nearly enough. She wanted to feel the work roughened skin of his fingers and palms caressing over her naked flesh.

She shook when Major began to kiss his way up the inside of her thighs as his hands continued to smooth up and down the outside of her legs. Her womb and pussy clenched reflexively seeking relief from the burning intensity making her insides throb.

She was so wet and needy she was sure Major would be able to see the patch of cream soaking her panties.

Ace broke the kiss, and while she wanted to demand he come back, she was too breathless to voice her desires.

She shivered with lusty heat when Rocco shoved his hands under her tank and caressed over her belly and up her torso. She held her breath as she waited for him to give her some reprieve from the yearning need to have her breasts touched without any barriers, but he stopped just at the undersides.

"You are so fucking beautiful, baby," Major signed. "We need to get your clothes off. Okay?"

She sucked in another breath and nodded quickly. She was too hungry to be worried about exposing her body to men's eyes for the first time. Liquid heat pooled low in her belly and she wanted to demand that they hurry up.

Goosebumps raced over her skin when Rocco gripped her arms and lifted them above her head. She turned to look at him over her shoulder and gasped when she met his blazing, hungry gray-green gaze. He kept their eyes locked as he skimmed his hands back down her arms and sides until he was holding the edge of her tank. And then he started tugging her shirt up in a slow, sensual slide over her skin.

She shivered and trembled with lust, and while she tried to keep the shudders from showing, she knew they'd all seen and felt her trembling.

"You aren't afraid of us are you, baby?" Major frowned.

She shook her head and then held her breath when his pupils dilated even further. She read about passion making a person's eyes change and glaze with need, but she'd never thought to see such things herself.

Delta was excited and trepidatious all at once, and while she was nervous, since she had no experience, she was eager for more. Eager to experience everything with these three men—the three men who managed to make her feel more than she'd ever felt in her whole life. And it wasn't just physical attraction.

Delta realized in that moment that she was in danger of falling in love with them.

Even though she'd dreamed of having a happy ever after like any other woman, she'd never expected to have one for herself. Feeling so much for Major, Rocco, and Ace scared the absolute shit out of her, but there wasn't a chance in hell she was going to walk away.

This moment, these three men, could be all she'd ever dreamed of, and she wasn't going to stop them just when they were starting.

For all she knew they could turn away from her once they had what they wanted. She mentally shook her head. She felt guilty for even thinking such things about them. They'd already proven they were noble men with good morals.

Delta realized that she was trying to talk herself out of going further, but she be damned if she'd listen to that cautious inner voice anymore.

This was her chance at liberation and she wasn't going to pass it up no matter what the consequences were.

Chapter Ten

Major hooked his thumbs into the side of her cotton boy shorts at the same time as Rocco tugged the tank top over Delta's head. His breath hitched in his throat when her gorgeous breasts came into view. They were so fucking beautiful his mouth watered for a taste, but when he was finally able to breathe again, he inhaled deeply and groaned as the musky scent of her sweet honey invaded his nostrils.

Ace leaned up and slanted his mouth over hers just as Rocco cupped her lush breasts in his hands. Her moan of pleasure was muffled as her tongue tangled with Ace's. She whimpered when Rocco began to knead and mold her breasts before strumming his thumbs over the hard, dusky rose-hued nipples.

If he wasn't so hungry for a taste of her he would have sat back and watched as his brothers pleasured their woman, but he was shaking with need and didn't want, couldn't, wait a moment longer.

He shoved his thumbs further down the side of her boy short panties, gave a hard tug and sighed with relief when the seams tore. He pulled the material out from under her ass and lowered his gaze to her pussy.

His heart rate escalated even more when he saw bare pink folds with drops of creamy dew glistening on her skin, and her clit was already so engorged the hood had already slid back.

With slow deliberation, he caressed his way up the inside of her thighs giving her time to protest and change her mind, all the while holding his breath and hoping she didn't.

When he reached the junction of her thighs, he lightly caressed over her labia majora and groaned when the tips of his fingers slid through her honey.

He glanced up to see that she was still kissing Ace passionately, and Rocco was pinching and plucking her nipples between his fingers and thumbs.

Major shifted on his knees and lowered down to his haunches until his mouth was hovering over her dripping cunt. He drew in another deep breath, taking the aroma of her cream deep into his lungs, and then lowered his head as he wrapped his arms around her upper thighs.

He took a long slow lick from her dripping hole to her protruding clit, loving the way she jerked as his tongue lapped over her nub and the moaning gasping sounds she made, but it still wasn't enough. Major wanted to hear her screaming in ecstasy.

This time instead of caressing over her clit with the flat of his tongue, he used the very tip to flick over her distended pearl rapidly. She groaned and whimpered and shoved her hips toward his face.

He tightened his hold around her legs, and then rimmed her creamy well with the tip of his finger as he swirled his tongue around her sensitive bud. Her legs shook in his hold, but he was holding her too tightly for her to escape him. Not that she was trying to pull away from him. In fact, the opposite was true. She was rocking her hips to and fro, and from the way Rocco was hissing and groaning, he was having a hell of a time staying in control. He gazed up Delta's body to see his brother grinding his teeth together and his head thrown back as if he was in pain. Each time Delta rocked, she had to be rubbing her sexy peach of an ass against Rocco's hard cock.

Major closed his eyes and savored each tremor of her body as he ate at her pussy. He licked down and lapped up her sweet honey before moving back to her clit to nibble on the small bud with his lips.

When he felt her entrance pulse open, he slipped his finger into her hole. He was the one groaning when her wet cunt clamped down around his digit. She was so fucking wet she was dripping, but she was also hot, and very, very tight. Almost too tight. He didn't need to be a genius to figure out that Delta had limited experience in the sex department, or that maybe she was still a virgin.

His heart and soul surged with protectiveness and possessiveness.

Although he could have paused things to ask her the all-important question, he didn't want to take time out from tasting her, and he didn't want her to feel self-conscious if she was inexperienced. There was a chance she would call everything to a halt, and he didn't want to give her a reason to change her mind. So he vowed then and there to make sure she only felt pleasure at his and his brothers' hands. However, he also wanted to stretch her out and make her come before taking her virginity. Major and his brothers were bigger than average and their cocks were no exception.

Pushing his thoughts aside, he began to pump his finger in and out of her cunt as he suckled and lapped at her clit. He couldn't wait to taste her cum in his mouth.

* * * *

Delta was on sensation overload. She was burning up and aching so badly she wanted to scream, but she since she didn't know how loud she'd be if she did, she swallowed the urge back down.

She couldn't believe what they were doing to her.

Major was licking her pussy and finger fucking her at the same time. Ace kept alternating between kissing her voraciously and nibbling and licking along her neck and nipping at her ear. Rocco was playing with her breasts, and each time he squeezed her nipples between his fingers and thumbs, her pussy clenched and her clit throbbed.

Her muscles were trembling and shaking, and her insides had a deep primal ache she didn't think would ever be appeased.

She groaned and gasped when Major added another finger to her pussy and began to pump them in and out. There were so many nerve endings inside her vagina, she felt as if she was about to break apart. The fire was consuming her from the inside out, and no matter how hard she tried to stay still, it wasn't possible.

She rolled her head back and forth on Rocco's chest, and while she tried to move her legs, Major had a good hold on them.

Each time Major stroked his fingers into her pussy, exquisite pressure grew inside her womb, pussy and clit. She felt as if she was about to burst apart and found herself straining toward the release she'd read so much about.

Just as she thought she was about to go over, Ace broke the kiss, Rocco stopped plucking at her nipples, and Major stilled his fingers in her pussy and lifted his mouth from her clit.

She drew in ragged breath after ragged breath and tried to quell the trembling in her limbs as she wondered why they'd stopped. She was about to ask what was wrong, but as she opened her eyes and met Major's hungry gaze, the question on the tip of her tongue fled.

The muscles in his face were tight with lust and his gray-blue eyes were glazed over with passion. Her gaze wondered over his broad shoulders, and chest and his muscular arms. He was pumped. His veins were standing up under his bronzed skin and she could see the tendons straining as well. She met his gaze again and gasped at the primal animalistic expression she found there. That was when she realized he was so hungry for her he was taking a few moments to calm down. Feminine confidence surged into her heart and soul. She had never affected anyone in her life, but seeing Major right on the edge sent power coursing through her veins.

She glanced up at Rocco to see the same expression on his face, and then she shifted her gaze to Ace. She was the one gasping this time. Ace was lying on his side on the bed with his head propped up on his hand and elbow and he was totally naked. She shivered when she followed the movement of his hand as he caressed down over his chest and belly toward his groin.

Her mouth went dry and she licked her lips when she saw him wrap his hand around the base of his shaft before pumping up and down a few times. Saliva flooded her mouth and she had to swallow to avoid choking and making a fool of herself. She'd read about oral sex of course, and while it had turned her on as her imagination went rife, Delta had honestly thought it was all a myth. Major had already proven her wrong, and now she wanted to return the favor. She wanted to wrap her own hand around Ace's long, thick, hard cock to feel if the skin was as soft as the books said, but most of all she wanted to lap up that clear bead of moisture glistening in the top of his small slit.

Delta lifted her hand about to reach out toward Ace, but she didn't get the chance.

Major lowered his head to her pussy and lapped at her clit as he thrust his finger in and out of her sheath, harder, faster and deeper.

Rocco kneaded her breasts before pinching her nipples between his fingers and thumb as he sucked and licked up and down the outside of her neck. This time there was no slow build up. The coil inside tautened faster than lightning, and before she knew it, she was hovering on the edge of release once more.

She moaned as she rolled her head back and forth on Rocco's chest, and when she felt a hand cup her cheek she didn't need to open her eyes to know that Ace was holding her face. He slanted his mouth over hers, his tongue gliding along and then twirling around hers.

And then she was screaming.

Nirvanic pleasure imploded deep in her womb, rippling out in concentric circles to her cunt and clit. Her internal muscles clamped and released, clenched and let go, over and over. Cream dripped from her pussy as she quaked and quivered in euphoric bliss.

All the time she was coming, Major continued pumping his fingers in and out of her pussy, while sucking and licking at her clit, wringing every last drop of pleasure from her depths.

The orgasm was so intense she saw stars, and though it felt as if the bliss lasted a lifetime, it was over way too soon. She slumped back against Rocco and tried to calm her breathing as aftershocks continued to wrack her body.

Major was kissing the inside of her thighs, and when he eased his fingers from her pussy, she moaned. She was so sensitive it was almost painful. She whimpered when he licked over her creamy hole and then shivered when the tip of his tongue penetrated her.

Delta opened her eyes to gaze down at Major and shook as another aftershock shuddered through her. His eyes were half closed and she knew he was making sounds because she could feel the vibrations against her sensitive vagina. She just hoped that he liked how she tasted, because she was definitely up for a lot more oral sex. When he shoved his fingers into his mouth and sucked them clean, she figured he must really like her juices, otherwise he wouldn't have done that.

She kept her eyes locked with his as he gained his feet, and then she was perusing his body up and down. He and his brothers were so fit and muscular they took her breath away. They were also the most good looking men she'd ever encountered, and not just because of their handsome visages. Their kindness and caring made them handsome to her no matter what they looked like.

When she saw how his huge erection was straining the fabric of his knit boxers, her just sated libido started to smolder again. She just hoped when it came time to make love with them, she wouldn't cry out in pain.

Major nudged her gaze back up to his. "Are you okay, baby? Are you ready for more?"

Delta wished she could shout hell yes like one of the heroines she'd read about in the erotic romance novels, but she was used to being without her voice.

"I'm fine, and yes, I'm ready for more."

She glanced down when she saw his hands move and her heart flipped when he hooked his thumbs into the waistband of his boxers and shoved them down.

She held her breath and bit her tongue to hold in her gasp of awe. His cock looked as if it was as thick as her wrist, and it was so long, the tip was level with his navel. The head was a reddish-purple color and the vein underneath was easily visible under the surface of his skin. When his cock flexed, she couldn't stop herself from reaching out and touching it.

She caressed the length of his hard dick up and down with the tips of her fingers, gasping over how hot it was. The skin was as smooth and as soft as she'd read about, and she gazed up at him as she slowly wrapped her hand around his shaft. She was in no way surprised when her fingers didn't meet, and then she began to stroke him.

Delta felt a little awkward and inept at her first attempts in pleasuring a man, and hadn't noticed she'd lowered her gaze to watch what she was doing until Rocco began to lick and nibble over her shoulder.

She lifted her gaze to Major and was glad to see he had his head thrown back and his lips parted as if he was gasping for breath. When she saw his chest rising and falling rapidly, she realized he was panting, and couldn't stop the smile from curving her lips.

Major lowered his gaze to hers, smiled back, and then clasped her wrist in his hand and tugged her to her feet. She was aware of movement behind her but her attention was wholly centered on him, right now.

"I need you, baby," he said. "I need to make love with you."

"I need you, too, Major." Delta gasped when he scooped her up into his arm and carried her closer to the bed. He lowered her down in the center of the mattress and followed her down.

She had no idea where Ace and Rocco were, but before she could sight them, Major slanted his mouth over hers, blocking everything and everyone else out.

His knee nudged hers and she didn't hesitate to widen her legs. She moaned when he settled between her splayed thighs. His hard cock was pressed against her mound and she wiggled her hips trying to get his erection to go where she was aching to have it.

Major released her lips and gazed into her eyes when she opened them. He was leaning his upper body weight on one elbow and his free hand was caressing up and down her side. Goosebumps raced over her heated skin in the wake of his gentle touch. She couldn't believe how wonderful it was to have his large, callused hand skimming over her flesh. Yet now that she'd had a taste of ecstasy, she wanted more.

"I need you," she mouthed.

His eyes glazed over even more and his pupils were so large there was only a thin rim of his gray-blue iris around them.

"I need you, too, baby. So much," he said.

He kept his eyes locked to hers as he scooted down a little. She moaned when he cupped and lifted one of her breasts with his hand. A sob of need escaped from between her parted lips when he laved the flat of his tongue over the hard, throbbing peak. And then she cried out when he sucked her nipple into his mouth.

It was so good she couldn't take it, yet she craved more and more. Each lick and suckle on her nipple sent zings of pleasure shooting straight down to her pussy, causing her clit to throb and her muscles to clench. Juices wept from her hole down over her ass and toward the sheets underneath her.

She'd had no idea her body could produce so much moisture, and while she probably should have been embarrassed, she was far from it. She was too hot, too needy, too hungry to worry about something like that right now.

Delta needed Major filling her like she needed her next breath. If he didn't get inside of her soon, she might just end up screaming.

She rolled her head back and forth on the pillow restlessly and threaded her fingers into his hair before trying to tug him back up. He lifted his head from her breast, winked at her, and then took her other nipple into his mouth.

He twirled his tongue around the areola and then flicked the nipple with the tip of his tongue. She moaned, bent her knees and pressed her feet into the mattress, needing leverage to bow her hips up toward his.

She shivered and cried out when he pressed her nipple up against the roof of his mouth, arching her chest up off the bed.

Major released her nipple and then shifted back up until his head was level with hers. She gasped in a deep breath just before he kissed her. There was no tentative brushing of lips this time. He devoured her mouth as if he was starving and she devoured him right back.

Their tongues tangled and twirled, glided and slid. Their teeth nipped at lips and then eased the sting. They breathed together, and if she wasn't mistaken their hearts were racing at the same pace. She could feel his heart thudding in time with hers. Delta felt as if he was consuming her, but she was consuming him right back.

He broke the kiss and she whimpered with pleasure when the tip of his cock pressed against her clit. She wrapped her arms around his neck and held on.

When she felt the broad bulbous head of his erection against her entrance, she held her breath and tried to relax, but it was impossible. She was tense with a blazing hungry need and didn't think she'd ever be able to relax again.

She opened her eyes when he stroked a finger down her nose, and had to blink him into focus since he was so close. When she saw his lips move she lowered her gaze to his mouth.

"Take a breath for me, baby. Relax. I'll go nice and slow. Okay?"

Delta nodded, which was in contradiction to her thoughts. She wanted to tell him to hell with slow and to hurry up, but she wasn't a masochist. This was her first time and his erection was big—she just hoped it wasn't big enough to cause her pain, but if it was, she prayed she wouldn't cry out or start weeping.

Her legs trembled when he breached her. The wet, delicate tissues of her pussy burned slightly as they stretched to accommodate his penetration.

Major lowered his head to her neck, licking and sucking at her skin. She moaned when he nipped at a sensitive spot just beneath her ear and shuddered when he continued to lap at the sweet spot.

She clung to his shoulders, hoping she wasn't hurting him with her blunt nails, but she couldn't seem to make herself ease up on her grip.

Major lifted his head from her neck, met her gaze briefly and slanted his mouth over hers.

Delta closed her eyes, groaning and gasping as they kissed each other ravenously and he stroked into her wet pussy a little deeper. Her pussy rippled and clenched around his invading cock and she felt him moan, the vibrations reverberating against her chest.

There was a little pain since her muscles were tight and untried, but the friction of his cock sliding in and out her pussy far outweighed the discomfort. He broke the kiss when he was all the way inside of her, allowing her to gasp much needed air into her burning lungs, and he once more met her gaze.

"Okay?" he asked.

She nodded, eager for more.

And then he began to pump his hips.

* * * *

Major felt as if he was touching heaven on earth.

Delta's pussy was so hot, wet and tight, he wasn't sure he was going to last the distance. It was only by sheer determined will alone that he hadn't already come deep inside of her. He'd had to stop often as she breached her virgin cunt, worried he was hurting her when he saw her grimace of pain. He'd realized she was trying to hide her discomfort from him and he would talk to her about that later. However, right now he needed to make love to his woman. To show her the joys of sex with someone you cared about, and he definitely cared about his woman. She'd already managed to get under his skin and into his heart and soul. Now that he was making love to her, making her his, he was never going to let her go.

When he was sure he could move without losing control, he drew back until just the tip of his cock was in her entrance, and then he slowly surged back in. She gasped and moaned, digging her nails into his shoulders, and he loved it. Loved that she was so overwhelmed with pleasure that she wasn't aware of what she was doing.

His primal caveman came roaring to the surface, and he wished the indents she was making in his skin would remain forever so he could wear them with pride.

He pushed his Neanderthal thoughts aside and retreated again.

Each time he drew back and drove into her, he increased the pace and depth, and when he felt his cock nudging the entrance to her womb, he hoped he wasn't hurting her. He opened eyes, which he hadn't realized he'd closed, and sighed with relief when all he saw was pure bliss on her face. The creamy skin of her cheeks was flushed and when he gazed lower, he wasn't surprised that her chest was a rosy hue, too.

When he felt the base of his spine begin to tingle he knew he was going to have to ramp up her pleasure and fast.

Major shifted up onto his knees, hooked his arms under her legs and began to rock faster. He had to grind his teeth when his balls grew hotter and harder, and he glanced over his shoulder at his brothers a little frantically. They'd taken up residence on the two-seater sofa against the back wall to give him space with their woman, but right now he needed their help. He wanted them kissing and caressing her while he loved on her, until she was screaming with orgasm.

Ace and Rocco rose and hurried toward the bed. They got up onto the mattress on either side of Delta and started caressing and kissing her. Rocco took her mouth and Ace began to suck and knead at her breasts.

Major dipped his finger into the wealth of cream coating her folds and then began to rub over her clit. She cried out loudly and he loved that she was so uninhibited with him as he made love to her.

He pumped his hips harder, faster, his cock hilting each time he surged forth. He applied more pressure to her clit and groaned when her cunt rippled along and around his hard dick.

Delta's eyes opened wide as did her mouth, and then she was screaming loudly.

Her body shook and shuddered, her pussy grabbed and released. The warmth tingling at the base of his lower back turned into a consuming fire that shot from his toes all the way up to his head.

His cock pulsed and thickened even more. His balls drew up close to his body and then blazing heat spewed from the tip of his cock with a roar. He ground his hips against hers as juices spumed fast and hard from his balls and out of his cock. Major had never felt anything so strong, so profound in his life. The top of his head felt as if it was about to burst open, but it was the roiling emotions in his too full heart and soul that almost did him in.

He didn't remember slumping down on top of Delta, but knew he was when he felt her chest trying to expand under his heavy weight. He knew he should lever up to let her fill her lungs properly, but his body was quaking and for the first time in his life he had no strength left in his muscles. He didn't even know where his brothers were. He was deaf and blind to everything but his woman, aftershocks still wracking them both.

Finally, his breathing began to slow and blood started coursing through his veins again. The quivering stopped and he braced his hands on the mattress on either side of Delta's head and lifted his upper body weight from her.

He stared in awe and wonder at her beautiful face. Her skin was glowing in the aftermath of their lovemaking, and while her eyes were closed, the soft, sultry smile on her face filled him with masculine pride. He'd held out just long enough to make her come, and he hoped he would be able to spend the rest of his life loving her and making her smile just like that over and over.

Major leaned down and kissed her softly on the lips. She blinked her eyes open and locked gazes with him.

"You're amazing, baby." He was glad she couldn't hear his voice, because it sounded low and raspy even to his own ears.

"No, I'm just me. That was…beautiful." She blinked rapidly when moisture filled her eyes and drew in a shaky breath.

"Yes, it was." He cupped her face between his hands and eased his softening cock from the tight, wet confines of her body.

She moaned and he groaned. He slipped to her side and then pulled her into his arms. She sighed and rested her head in the crook of his arm and shoulder. She caressed a hand over his chest, her fingers threading through his chest hair.

In that moment, he wanted to ask her to marry him and his brothers, but knew it was way too soon.

Hopefully, in a few months he would be able to pop the question and she'd say yes.

Chapter Eleven

Leo stood in the alley across the street and watched the sheriffs as they tried to gather evidence. He snorted softly at the wasted time, but the law wouldn't know he wasn't stupid enough to leave prints behind. He nearly always had gloves with him, since they protected his hands from being damaged too much while working. Wood could leave splinters behind, and while he wasn't a wuss, he wasn't stupid either. He'd had a few deep splinters he'd had to cut from his skin, hence the gloves.

He was also pissed. Pissed that he'd been interrupted while trying to get to the deaf cunt who'd been responsible for his brother's death. He had no idea how she'd called for reinforcements, or even how she'd known he was there, but she had. Maybe the bitch wasn't as stupid as he thought. How was he supposed to know if she was dumb as well as deaf and mute? She never seemed to venture out of the diner's kitchen, let alone anywhere else.

When he'd seen those three men coming to the rescue along with the sheriffs, his first instinct had been to go back to his truck and follow them, but that would have been as if he'd painted a bullseye on his forehead. The men in this small Colorado town weren't stupid, and much to his surprise, they were all pussy whipped. He couldn't believe how protective they were of anyone weaker. He was going to have to be really careful and plan out what to do next.

If any of the men in town got wind of why he was here or what he was up to, he had a feeling he'd be a dead man, just like his brother. So far, he'd been able to fly under the radar, but one slip up could put him in the spotlight.

He might have to wait longer than first anticipated, but in the end, he would get what he wanted.

Revenge on that cunt for getting his brother killed.

* * * *

Rocco and Ace had rolled from the bed the moment Delta was close to climax. Now that Major had staked a claim and made love to their woman, Rocco wanted to have his turn. Nonetheless, he would give his brother and their woman all the time they needed to bond. Plus, he was concerned that she would be too sore for anymore lovemaking. In the end, Major had taken her hard and fast and she was bound to be tender. If he needed to wait for another day to make love with Delta, then he would.

Major kissed Delta on the forehead and rolled from the bed before standing and heading into the adjoining bathroom. Rocco glanced at Ace and they both rose and walked toward Delta. Her eyes widened for a second and he wondered if she was afraid of them, but when her gaze eyed their bodies over and a spark of heat lit her green-hued orbs, he pushed that ludicrous thought aside.

"How are you feeling, honey?" Rocco signed as well as asked verbally just in case he fucked up.

A slow smile curved her kiss swollen red lips up. "Wonderful." She patted the mattress on either side of her and he sighed with relief. He was thankful she hadn't told him and Ace to leave her alone.

Major came back from the bathroom and tossed a damp cloth at him. Rocco caught it and then tapped Delta's thigh. "Spread your legs, honey. Let me clean you up."

Her eyes widened again and then she shook her head. "I can do it."

Ace cupped her face to gain her attention. "You're our woman now darlin' and we take care of what's ours. Do as Rocco says."

"I'm not a possession."

Rocco drew back, his heart aching with pain. He couldn't believe she would think such a thing.

"Major, we need you to stay and interpret. Maybe she didn't read me right."

Delta pushed herself up and scooted back toward the bedhead, bringing her knees up toward her body and hugging her legs with her arms. "I didn't misunderstand."

Major kneeled on the end of the bed and signed quickly. Rocco was glad his brother also spoke out loud so he and Ace knew what he was saying.

"The men of his town are different, baby. We like seeing to our woman's needs no matter what they are. We don't think of you as a possession and never will, but now that you've agreed to be in a relationship with us, you are our responsibility."

Delta frowned. "No one is responsible for another adult. Everyone is responsible for themselves."

"You're right," Ace replied. "However, the men in this town are very protective and possessive. We don't care what other people think of us, but we will always make sure you are happy, safe, and comfortable."

"That means we will clean you up after making love with you. We will make sure you eat regularly and adhere to the rules that are set out," Rocco explained.

"Rules? I don't need rules. I'm not a child." Delta glared at him.

"No, you're not," Major said. "The men of this town involved in polyandrous relationships have had to protect their women from danger. They've been on the run from abusive as well as evil murdering men. Add in the prejudice the women have had to deal with when the first few ménage relationships formed, well, you can imagine how well that went over. The sheriffs and the men set out rules to help keep the women and children safe. It's not that we're arrogant controlling assholes, baby, we just need to make sure that our women and kids are safe."

"What's that got to do with this?" Delta asked then pointed at the wash cloth.

"We want you to be comfortable, honey," Rocco said.

"You have no need to be embarrassed, darlin'." Ace took her hand in his and squeezed gently. "We've seen everything there is to see."

Delta lowered her head and while her cheeks were still tinged pink, she lifted her eyes again, and met each of their gazes. "I'm not used to it, though."

Rocco bit his tongue to keep a grin from curving his lips. He couldn't believe how shy their woman was after making love with Major. She'd been so uninhibited while in the throes of passion, he couldn't wait to see her that way again, but this time while she was making love with him.

He leaned forward and brushed his lips over hers. Rocco groaned when she opened to him immediately. Her arms moved from around her knees to loop around his neck, and when she straightened her legs, he hooked an arm around her waist and tugged her down the mattress.

He delved into her mouth, sliding his tongue along and around hers, inhaling her scent into his lungs and savoring her taste. She moved closer to him, pressing the front of her body against his. Her hard, little nipples brushed against his chest and then stabbed into his skin. He moaned and she whimpered. When she lifted one of her legs and slung it over his hip, he took the opportunity to clean her up with the damp cloth. She gasped as he wiped over her sensitive folds, but he was glad she didn't baulk or protest, but instead kissed him hungrily.

He felt the mattress move and forced his passion-heavy lids up to see Ace had moved in behind Delta. He closed his eyes again, flung the cloth over his shoulder to the floor, and then caressed up and down her side.

Rocco broke the kiss before licking and nipping his way down to her chest. Her neck arched as she threw her head back until it thudded against Ace's chest. He pressed against her shoulder, pushing both her and Ace over until his brother was lying on his back and she was half reclining on top of him. He cupped both her breasts in his hands, taking time to knead and mold her soft, silky, supple flesh. She gasped and groaned when he thrummed his thumbs over the hard peaks and then arched up into his hands when he squeezed her nipples between his fingers and thumbs.

Ace was kissing and licking at the side of her neck while smoothing his hands up and down her sides. When her legs began to move restlessly, Rocco knew the smoldering embers were beginning to flame hotter and brighter.

His cock was so hard it was aching and he could feel moisture bubbling to the tip of his dick. He wasn't sure how much longer he could go without burying himself deep inside her sexy body, but he needed to make sure she was wet and ready. There was no way in hell he was causing her pain just because he was overeager.

Rocco tugged her away from Ace, grasped her hips and flipped her over onto her stomach. Delta gasped with shock and glanced at him over her shoulder. He tugged on her hips, pulling her up onto her hands and knees and nodded to his brother.

Ace scooted into the middle of the bed, pushing his legs in under Delta's body.

"Is she shocked?" Rocco asked.

Ace nudged Delta's gaze up toward his with a finger under her chin. "No, she looks hungry. She's licking her lips while staring at my cock."

"Make sure she's okay with this, Ace," Rocco rasped out.

"I have to get her gaze off my cock—Oh, fuck yeah." Ace groaned.

"She's fucking amazing." Rocco ran his hands up and down Delta's back and squeezed her ass cheeks. She was licking at Ace's cock with her ass higher in the air. He hoped she liked having her ass played with, but he would soon find out.

Rocco released her butt cheeks and caressed up and down her folds. She gasped and groaned when he rubbed light circles over her clit and then dipped into her soaked pussy.

"She's dripping with cream."

"Ah shit!" Ace gasped as he threaded his fingers into Delta's hair.

Rocco moved in closer behind her and curved his front over her back. He was just in time to see their woman suck Ace's cock into her mouth. "She's so fucking sexy. So passionate."

"Hell yes, she is." Ace made a weird gurgling sound before meeting his gaze. "You'd better get inside of her fast, bro. She's sucking me like a pro."

"Don't fucking say that."

"You know I'm not trying to be derogatory. What I meant was that she's naturally passionate." Ace sucked in a deep breath and then tugged on Delta's hair.

She released his cock with a loud pop and lifted her gaze to Ace's. "You have to stop, darlin'."

She shook her head and was about to take Ace's cock back into her mouth, but Rocco wrapped and arm around her waist and tugged her back toward him. He spread the cream coating her folds, stroked over her clit, and then aligned his cock with her entrance.

He stilled and grit his teeth as soon as the tip of his dick breached her hot, tight, wet cunt. The urge to shove into her hard and fast was almost too strong to ignore, but he resisted. However, when she pushed back against him, he nearly lost it. Her internal muscles clamped around his cock as he sank in another inch or so. He tightened his hold on her waist to hold her still.

"Fuck. So responsive. Play with her nipples. You need to distract her for me."

"That good?" Ace asked.

"Better."

Ace reached under her and from the way her pussy clamped around him and she moaned, Rocco knew his brother was plucking at her nipples.

He drew back and began to stroke slowly in and out of her pussy, loving the way she soaked him in her cream and how her tight muscles pulsed around his hard, aching cock.

Rocco inhaled the sweet musky scent of her honey and her natural pheromones. Never had a woman smelled as good, as right as Delta did. His heart was full of warmth and emotions he never felt before. He hadn't realized how cold and numb he was until she came into their lives, and now that she was in his and his brothers bed, he had no intention of letting her go.

Ever.

When Rocco felt her pussy begin to swell inside, he knew she was ready for more. He shifted upright onto his knees, gripped her hips and began to love her in earnest. He drew back and then powered forward until he was buried inside of her to the root before retreating again.

She whimpered and gasped, moaned and groaned each time he pressed deep and withdrew. He increased the pace, depth, and strength of his thrusts until his pubis and thighs were slapping against her butt and the back of her thighs.

Each time he embedded his cock to the hilt, she soaked him with her juices until they were dripping from his balls.

When he felt the warning tingle at the small of his back he knew he wasn't going to last long. "Rub her clit."

Ace shifted his legs out from under her body and then reclined on his back across the bed, his head under Delta's chest. He sucked one of her nipples into her mouth and then reached down toward her pussy.

"Oh," Delta moaned, her cunt muscles rippling along the length of his dick.

Rocco couldn't take much more. He pistoned his hard cock in and out of her pussy, and after licking his thumb, pressed it against her star.

Delta tensed, stopped breathing and froze, but when he applied more pressure on her asshole, air exploded from her lungs as she groaned loudly.

The heat in his lower back spread around toward his groin and into his balls. His balls hardened and lifted up toward his body. Rocco drove in hard before pulling back and shoving in hard again. Delta began to shake and he could feel tension invading her cunt muscles as she drew closer to climax, but he was about to go over, too.

Rocco pressed harder on her pucker, breaching her ass with the tip of his thumb and slammed into her again and again. A deep guttural sound emitted from her mouth just before she started screaming.

Her cunt clamped around him so hard, it was difficult to continue sliding his cock in and out of her pussy, but he didn't stop. He wanted to wring every little bit of her orgasm out of her until she couldn't hold herself up anymore.

Rocco shifted on his knees and surged back in deep, making sure the head of his dick rubbed over her G-spot and sent her careening straight back up into another climax. She shook and shivered, bathing him with her cum as it gushed from her body.

His balls were on fire and he shouted as he drove in deep and froze. Blazing liquid heat shot up from his balls, along his dick and out of the top of his penis as he climaxed. A ringing set up in his ears and white streaks of light passed in front of his eyes and he came and came and came. His mind, body and soul seemed to shoot up into the stratosphere, and although he could see the entire universe with an astounding clarity, he only had eyes for Delta.

She was the everything to him. The air he breathed, the reason his heart beat, the love of his life. Everything he'd had to endure before meeting her was worth it just so he could hold her in his arms, make love with the one woman meant to be his and his brothers.

All the pain and violence he'd seen while fighting for his country fled. His cold, empty heart filled with so much warmth and love, it overflowed. His soul, which had been so numb, so unfeeling, came roaring back to life.

He didn't care if she thought them over the top with their rules and regulations. Those rules had been set up to keep the women and children of Slick Rock safe and secure. She'd get used to them eventually.

Rocco would do anything to keep her safe and happy even if that meant spanking her ass.

When his breathing started to even out he blinked his gaze into focus and eased his semi-flaccid cock from her pussy. He sat back on his bent legs pulling her with him. She leaned against his chest as she panted for breath and gazed up at him over her shoulder.

He combed his fingers into her hair and kissed her, passionately, lovingly, and hoped she came to love him and his brothers as much as he loved her.

Rocco released her lips and then kissed each of her eyelids, her nose, her forehead, and then her lips again. She opened her eyes and met his gaze. His heart lurched at what he saw in those beautiful jade green eyes.

Delta might not love him yet, but she was definitely starting to care for him.

However, deep down in his subconscious he was worried for her safety.

Someone had broken into the diner and destroyed the place. What filled him with fear was how the fucker had tried to get to their woman.

He and his brothers were going to have to work with the sheriffs and see if they could find out who was after Delta. Maybe the security cameras had picked up something before the power had been cut.

They were going to have to meet up with the Alcott brothers. He mentally cursed himself for not thinking about that when Giles had called to apologize. If he had, the sheriffs could have already arrested the bastard.

He chuffed out a frustrated breath. He was clutching at straws. Giles would have told him and his brothers if that had been the case and the asshole would have been arrested.

He pushed his thoughts aside when Delta caressed his cheek and then leaned up to kiss his lips. He could worry about all of that later. Right now, he needed to concentrate on his woman's needs.

He gently lifted her into his arms, gained his feet and carried her toward the bathroom. She had to be sore now and a soak in a hot bath would help ease any tenderness.

Ace rushed ahead of him, flicked the light on and turned the taps on.

Rocco sat on the edge of the tub with Delta sitting across his thighs.

"What's wrong?" she asked.

"Nothing's wrong, honey," he answered.

"Then why are you frowning?"

"I'm worried about you. You have to be tender."

She ducked her head when she started blushing but nodded in agreement.

Rocco lifted her gaze to his with a finger under her chin. "Ace will take care of you, Delta."

She glanced at Ace who was already sitting in the filling spa bath and nodded.

Rocco helped her into the tub and then headed to clean up in his own bathroom. After that he was going to search out Major and talk to him about the incident at the diner. He didn't like the idea of Delta staying there by herself after someone had broken in, but he had a feeling if they asked her to move in with them she would refuse.

"What the hell do we do now?" he asked himself as he stepped in under the hot water.

Chapter Twelve

"Come over here, darlin'," Ace said as he crooked a finger at her.

Delta slid along the seat in the spa and was grateful when Ace clasped her upper arms and lifted her into his lap.

She was so satiated her muscles felt like jelly and she wasn't sure she could bear her own weight. She sighed with contentment as she leaned back into his big, muscular body. The hot water felt wonderful on her stiff aching muscles, and while her pussy was feeling tender, it wasn't all that painful. She couldn't believe she'd made love to two men.

She felt as if her heart and soul was soaring free after breaking away from the shackles society had placed her in. Although she was happy about it, she couldn't understand why Major, Rocco, and Ace were attracted to her, but if she overthought things, she might end up destroying what they'd started and she didn't want that. Not when she had everything she'd dreamed about coming to fruition.

Ace cupped her chin and brought her gaze up to his. "How are you feeling, darlin'?" he asked as he signed.

She giggled when he signed the word house instead of feeling.

"What?"

She turned to face him so she was straddling his lap, very aware of his erection pressed against her mound when she got a little too close. She braced her hands on his biceps about to move back so she didn't hurt him, but he must have read the intentions in her eyes because he snagged an arm around her waist and pulled her tighter against him.

"Stay where you are, Delta. You're not hurting me. Now, tell me why you giggled."

She signed the word feeling and formed it on her lips. He copied her until she nodded to let him know he had it right.

"What did I ask you, then?"

Delta decided it was time to use the voice she couldn't hear. She'd had hours and hours of practice forming words with a speech therapist, and while she felt vulnerable and uncomfortable about speaking, she decided she couldn't hide out forever. Plus, if Ace, Major, or Rocco ever made fun of her, she would leave them without a backward glance.

Why did that thought make her heart ache?

But deep down she knew they would never do anything to deliberately hurt her, which was why she'd taken a chance on them, why she'd agreed to make love and try a relationship with them.

"You asked, how are you house, darlin'." She pressed the tips of two fingers to her voice box as she spoke.

Ace's eyes widened and his mouth gaped open as if he was in shock. When he didn't do or say anything, she felt shame and humiliation well up in heart and soul. Tears burned the back of her eyes and she was just about to push off his lap when he palmed her face between his hands.

"You spoke. You are so fucking amazing, darlin'. I can't believe you can talk. How did you learn when you can't hear?" He frowned as he stared into her eyes. "Why the hell are you crying?"

He turned his gaze toward the bathroom door and said something, but she had no idea what since she couldn't see his lips face on. She gripped his wrists and tried to pull his hands away from her face but he didn't let go.

She shoved to her feet and spun away from him just as the bathroom door burst open. Major and Rocco hurried toward her but she didn't want any of them touching her right now. She was so close to breaking down, if they so much as looked at her she would be crying up a storm.

Delta berated herself for being so gullible. She should have known not to get involved, that she would only end up embarrassing herself and heartbroken. How could she feel so much for them after knowing them for such a short time? And yet she did. The pain in her heart was so intense she wanted to double over and wail out her grief.

She took another step intending to sink into the water on the other side of the tub, but she didn't make it. The bottom was slick with water and soap from the bubbles Ace had put into the bath and her legs flew out from under her. She screamed as she began to fall and hoped she didn't hit her head on the side of the tub.

* * * *

"Fuck!" Ace surged to his feet and caught Delta before she fell into the water.

"What the fuck did you do?" Major asked angrily.

"You fucking made her cry," Rocco snarled.

"I don't know why she's so upset." Ace frowned. "I think something got lost in translation."

Ace stepped out of the tub, taking Delta with him, and after lowering her feet to the bath mat, he wrapped a towel around her. "Will you please find out why she's so upset?" He met Major's gaze.

Major nodded and sighed. He nudged her chin up and when Ace saw the tears rolling down her cheeks, his heart clenched painfully. He snagged a towel off the rail and wrapped it around his waist. "Wait, this is my doing. I need to be the one to sort it out."

Major nodded again and stepped back.

Ace moved closer to Delta and sighed with relief when she met his gaze. "I don't know what I did to hurt you, darlin', but I'm sorry. I would never want to make you cry. I was just so happy you could talk. I didn't think you could since all you've ever done is sign to us."

"You aren't repulsed by the sound of my voice or the way I say words?"

"What? Why the hell would you think that?" Ace asked, bewildered. "I think you have an amazing voice, Delta. It's soft and musical."

"Are you lying to me?"

He stared into her eyes and hoped she could see his sincerity. "I would never lie to you, darlin'. Honesty is paramount in any relationship, as is communication. I can promise you right here and now, that I will never, *ever*, lie to you."

She nodded and her shoulders dropped from around her ears as she relaxed again. "I'm sorry."

"You have nothing to be sorry for, Delta."

"I jumped to conclusions."

Ace breached the distance between them and tugged her into his arms. He kissed her forehead and drew back so she could see his lips. "You're human just like we are, honey. None of us are perfect. Hell, we're men and are likely to fuck up a time or two, but please, don't ever think me or my brothers would make fun of you. We care for you, Delta. Okay?"

"Okay," she answered verbally.

Major nodded at Ace and then he and Rocco left the room.

Ace wanted to know who'd told his woman she sounded funny when she spoke, and when he found out he was going to beat the shit out of the fucker, but right now he had a woman to love. By the time he was finished making her scream in pleasure, he was going to tell her how much he loved her.

He sighed with relief when she wrapped her arms around his waist and he just stood there holding her. He wished they didn't have the towels between them so he could feel her naked body pressed against his, but he would, needed, to be patient. Ace was determined to go at her pace even if it killed him.

She squeezed him before drawing back and then moved to the vanity and picked up the brush, which had been sitting there on the counter just waiting for her to use. It was brand new as was everything else in the master en suite. She met his gaze in the mirror, holding the brush up for him to see and quirked her eyebrow in query.

Ace moved up behind her, grasped her shoulders and turned her to face him. "No other woman or person has ever used this room or bathroom. Whatever is in here is yours, darlin'."

She frowned as her gaze drifted to the brush, back to him and to the brush again. "Why?"

"My brothers and I set this room up for the woman we were waiting for to complete us, honey. You're that woman."

Delta lowered the brush and her gaze. She shook her head before staring into his eyes. "You don't know that. You don't know me."

Ace nodded and palmed her cheeks. "I do, *we* do know that. We've never been attracted to another woman the way we're attracted to you, darlin'. I agree that we're still getting to know each other, have a lot to learn about each other, but I know, here"—he placed his hand on his chest over his heart—"that you are the woman we've been waiting for. The woman we can and want to spend the rest of our lives with."

"Why do you all want me?" she asked. "What if one or two of you find yourself attracted to someone else. What then?"

Ace shook his head. "We need to get dressed. Major and Rocco need to be present while we have this discussion."

She sighed and turned back toward the mirror and brushed her hair.

Ace didn't want her out of his sight. He was hot and horny but also feeling very possessive, but he needed to give her some time alone to think over what he'd already told her. Hopefully, he and his brothers could convince her that none of them would feel an attraction toward anyone else.

He rushed toward his bedroom for some clothes, cursing his hard on when he had trouble doing up his jeans. He had a feeling that his turn to make love with Delta had just been shot all to hell. If that was the case and his erection didn't subside he was going to have to take matters into his own hands, otherwise he wouldn't be getting any sleep in the near future.

* * * *

Although the need to make love and connect with Ace was a deep yearning in the pit of her gut, she wanted, needed answers to the questions she'd asked.

She wasn't biased and had been aware of the groups of men with one woman, but she hadn't thought anything of it. She didn't care how other people lived their lives, who or how they loved, but now that she was becoming involved with more than one man, she needed to know how they thought, how they felt.

Ever since she left the institution she had strict control over her life, over everything she did, and right now she felt as if she was at sea adrift with no way to steer. She'd always kept her distance from other people even while interacting with them so she wouldn't be hurt, and because of how others treated her just because she was a little different.

Right now, she was overwhelmed, her mind spinning off into a thousand different directions but going around in circles. When tension began to invade her muscles, she tried to clear her mind and grabbed some jeans and a light sweater. She didn't bother with shoes, because the floors were dark-stained hardwood and wasn't cold beneath her bare feet.

Once she was dressed she headed out toward the kitchen and hoped she wasn't, and hadn't, made the biggest mistake of her life. When her heart didn't flip or race with trepidation, she knew deep down in her gut that she hadn't, but she still needed to understand why three men wanted to share one woman.

She entered the living room to find Major, Rocco, and Ace sitting on the sofa. Warmth surged into her heart when they all stood up. They were gentlemen through and through. She hoped she got to meet the woman who'd instilled such good moralistic ethics into their beings.

"Come sit here, baby," Major signed before patting the cushion next to him.

She walked over and sat where he indicated. When he stood and moved away, she frowned but realized he was moving to sit on the edge of the coffee table in front of her so she could see him signing.

"Ace said you have a few questions," Major said.

Delta nodded, drew in a deep breath and asked her first question. "What if one or all of you find out you're attracted to another woman?"

Rocco shifted to face her. "That won't happen, honey."

Delta was glad that Major had moved because although Rocco was answering her and she was reading his lips, she could see Major signing from the corner of her eye.

"You don't know that."

Ace rose from his seat and sat next to Major. "Yes, we do, darlin. We've had plenty of experience with the opposite sex. We know when something is right. We aren't young kids."

"But—"

"There are no buts, baby," Major signed. "Do you think we pursue women the way we've pursued you? We don't give out our cell phone numbers to just anyone. You're beautiful, Delta. We were drawn to you from the start, and each minute we spend with you just makes us realize how right you are for us."

"What if you're not right for me?" She hated herself as soon as she asked that question. She had no idea why she was being so cruel. Tears burned her eyes and she lowered her gaze as guilt pierced her heart. She'd seen the flash of hurt in each of their gazes and wished she could take her question back.

Ace leaned forward and grasped her arms. He was angry with her and had every right to be. "Why would you ask that? Are you trying to pick a fight with us so you can leave? We know you wouldn't have agreed to make love with us, be with us, if you didn't have feelings for us." He released her arms, stood and began to pace.

While she tried to keep the tears from welling she lost the battle and they rolled down her face. She wrapped her arms around her waist and bent over.

Rocco scooped her up from the cushion and plonked her into his lap. He tilted her head back and gently wiped the tears from her cheeks. "What's this really about, honey?"

"I'm scared," she finally answered honestly.

"Of us?" He scowled at her.

"No. Yes. I don't know!"

"You don't think we'd hurt you, do you?"

"No."

"Then what are you so afraid of?" Major asked.

Since they'd been nothing but honest with her she decided she should be the same. "I'm scared of falling in love with you all and getting my heart broken."

Rocco tilted her gaze up toward his. "Life can be risky, honey, just as relationships can be. Do you think we would open ourselves up to you if we didn't think this was going to work? Are you going to spend the rest of your life scared of caring for someone in case you get hurt? You can't keep everyone at an arm's length forever, Delta. We're just as vulnerable as you are, honey, but we're willing to take the risk because we know deep in our hearts that you're worth it."

"I don't know what to do." Inside she was crying. Crying for the all those long lonely years behind her. Crying for the love already forming in her heart. Crying with need to be with them for the rest of her life, but she thought over Ace's words and knew he was right. If she wanted to have a chance at love and a normal life, she needed to open herself up and hold on tight. If she got her heart broken, at least she'd have tried and wouldn't have any regrets.

Major clasped one of her hands in his and Ace clasped the other. Rocco was stroking a hand up and down her back. She fell head over heels in love with them right then and there. Even after she'd hurt them with her careless words they were still trying to comfort her. They were putting her needs and emotions before their own because that was the type of men they were. Good, honorable, noble, kind hearted men, even if they would never admit it.

They'd told her they were emotionless, numb after fighting in the military. That was so far from the truth it was implausible.

All her concerns fled. The turmoil in her heart was replaced with full overflowing love for Major, Rocco, and Ace. None of them could predict the future, but she wasn't about to walk away from them because of fear. She'd never been a coward before and she wasn't going to start being one now.

She'd known when she'd agreed to make love with them and have a relationship that they'd somehow managed to work their way into her heart.

Delta realized that although they may look at and admire a member of the opposite sex, that they would never wander. If they fell in love with her the way she'd already fallen for them, they would never, ever stray. They would be loyal and love her for the rest of their days.

"You're all right," she said. "I've kept myself at a distance because it was easier than trying to prove to others I was just like them. It hurt me when people turned their back on me or gazed at me as if I was a bug under a microscope. I didn't even notice how isolated I kept myself until I needed to hire staff for the diner. I'm sorry for being such a coward."

"You could never be a coward, darlin'." Ace squeezed her hand. "Don't you know how much we admire you? You've spent your whole life dealing with narrow-minded bigots but here you are willing to take a chance on us, on life. That takes courage, Delta."

Delta had never looked at things from that perspective, nor had she realized that it took strength to not cave to what others expected. Lightness filled her heart and soul.

She hadn't even noticed that she still had some of those preconceived shackles from society holding her back. She'd been just as guilty as all those biased assholes for her loneliness, but now that the bonds had been stripped from her body and mind, she was going to live her life to the fullest. Happiness and love coursed through her veins and poured into her heart and soul.

It was time to face life head on instead of hiding from it.

Chapter Thirteen

Ace held his breath as the shadows in Delta's jade green eyes lightened. The frown which had been marring her face smoothed out and her lips curved up into one of the sexiest, sultriest smiles he'd ever seen a woman make.

She tugged her hands free from his and Major's and then rose. He followed the movement of her hands, and when she crossed her arms down low and gripped the hem of her sweater, the breath exploded from his lungs.

He wasn't sure if he blinked or maybe zoned out for a second, but when he was able to focus again, she'd already pulled her top off and flung it aside. His cock had gone down to half-mast while they'd been talking, but it roared back to full attention in less than a second.

He clenched his hands into fists to stop himself from reaching for her and pulling her into his arms. She needed to do this, needed to feel confident and sexy in her own feminine skin. How he knew that, he had no clue. He just did.

So, he remained seated on the coffee table, frozen like a statue with his gaze riveted to her sexy body.

When her fingers tugged the button on her jeans open, he clenched his jaw and tried to ignore his throbbing cock. He wanted to shift and relieve the tight pressure of his jeans on his aching erection, but he didn't want to distract Delta from her sexy strip tease.

The sound of her zipper lowering had his heart pounding against his ribs, and when she wriggled her hip as she shoved her jeans down, he began to sweat.

She kicked the jeans aside and waited, hoping she wouldn't chicken out and remove those little wisps of lace hiding her feminine attributes from his gaze.

Ace glanced at Rocco to see his brother staring at Delta's ass and he was licking his lips. When Major shifted beside him, for the first time in forever he was jealous of his brothers. Jealous that they'd each made love with their woman already and he hadn't. He wanted to have that with her, too. He wasn't envious of his brothers touching her or loving her. He just felt as if he was missing out by not having had his moment with her.

He wasn't sure if he'd portrayed that in his body language or maybe his eyes. He hoped he hadn't made her feel guilty because that was the last thing he wanted. However, he was human enough to be happy when she held her hand out to him and not either of his brothers. He clasped her hand and stood when she tugged. She stroked his cheek and then said, "I want you, Ace."

"I want you, too, darlin'."

She went up on tiptoes and he met her halfway. Her tongue licked over his lips, seeking entrance. He moaned as he opened to her. When her arms hooked around his neck, he caressed down her sides, gripped her ass and lifted her, turned and began walking toward the bedroom.

His heart filled with warmth and happiness, that she was already getting to know them. She was giving herself to him just as she had given herself to his brothers. He stopped at the end of the bed and lowered her feet to the floor. He kept his eyes locked with hers and quickly removed his clothes. Her gaze eyed his body over, and he groaned with hunger when she licked her lips while staring at his cock. He'd already felt her hot, wet mouth on his erection and couldn't wait to feel it there again, but right now he was too desperate to let her explore his body.

He moved into her until their bodies were touching, threaded his fingers into her hair, and slanted his mouth over hers. Her small, soft hands smoothed over his shoulder and down his arms. His blood heated and sweat sheened his skin. He caressed up her sides, over her arms and down her back. When he couldn't take another moment of the exquisite torture, he flicked open the clasp on her bra and swept the straps down her arms.

He released her lips, dragged air into his lungs, and lifted her into his arms and took her down to the mattress. Ace shifted to her side, so he wouldn't crush her smaller frame with his heavy weight, shoved his thumb beneath one side of her panties and pulled them down.

Delta sat up and took over the task of removing her undies. He could have stayed right where he was, staring at her sexy body for hours, if he hadn't been so hungry for her. Ace wouldn't be satisfied until she was screaming his name as she came apart in his arms.

* * * *

Delta was so hot for Ace she was shaking. Cream was leaking from her pussy and she was throbbing all over. She needed to have him inside of her now.

She rolled to her hands and knees and quickly straddled his hips and met his gaze. She'd always thought gray eyes were cold like steel, but his eyes were blazing hot with hunger and it was all for her.

As she bent down to kiss him, his hands moved over her body, caressing and cupping, inflaming the heat of her desire. Her pussy clenched with emptiness and the heated ache in her womb intensified. She needed to make love and connect with Ace on a physical and emotional level, and she didn't want to wait any longer.

She broke the kiss, gasped in a breath, and reached back to clasp his hot, thick, hard cock. She teased them both by moving the tip through her wet folds and groaned when the head pressed against her clit. When Ace gripped her hip firmly she realized he was gritting his teeth as if he was close to losing control.

When she sank down and took the tip of his cock into her hot, tight, wet body, he held his breath and clutched his fists into the sheets. He was about a hairsbreadth from flipping her over and pounding into her hard, fast and deep.

"Oh," she moaned and lifted up slightly before sinking back down and taking him in deeper.

His breath sawed in and out of his lungs and sweat began to roll down his temples. Pain and pleasure mingled together until he couldn't tell which way was up. Each and every muscle in his body tensed in preparation to move, to arch up into her until he was balls deep. The only reason he kept his tenuous control on a tether was because of the fear of hurting her.

She was new to love making and he didn't want to scare her with his hungry intensity, but he was strung so taut he felt as if he was about to snap.

He didn't realize how tightly he was holding the sheets until he heard them rip. He tried to think of something mundane to keep his animalistic instincts at bay, but his mind couldn't or wouldn't settle on any one thing. When the soft, silky skin of her thighs brushed against the top of his, and her pussy pressed against his pubis as she leaned forward, he broke.

Ace wrapped his arms around her waist, pulled her down on top of him and rolled until she was under him. She blinked at him with surprise and he was about to apologize, but when she smiled at him, he knew everything was all right. Would always be all right. How could it not when the love of his life was smiling up at him, desire glazing her eyes over, and there was so much emotion in those jade-green orbs, she took his breath away.

He braced his weight on his elbows and cupped her breasts, kneading the baby soft flesh before flicking her nipples with his thumbs. She moaned and arched up into him. He bent down, opened his mouth over hers and kissed her wildly, passionately, carnally. Their tongues danced and dueled, teeth nipped and tongues licked. When she wrapped her legs around his waist and dug her heels into her ass, he couldn't hold still any more.

Ace drew back until the head of his cock was just resting inside her entrance, and then he slowly surged forward again. Delta tilted her head back after releasing his lips and whimpered.

He watched every expression, heard and savored every moan and relished all of her tight, wet flesh enveloping his cock as he stroked into her over and over.

He licked and sucked on her neck, as he pumped his hips in and out of her hot, wet cunt. He knew the moment his cock brushed over her G-spot because her internal muscles clamped down on him and then rippled along his length. He groaned as she bathed his hard dick in her sweet, musky cream and shifted slightly higher onto his knees so that he would rub over that hot-spot every time he drove back into her.

Ace was set on having her screaming his name as she climaxed.

* * * *

Delta couldn't believe how emotionally connected she felt to Ace. She couldn't believe she'd been so bold as to make the first move, but she had newfound confidence and there was no way she was going to go back to that reserved, scared, little mouse.

Although she'd loved being in control for a while, she also liked that she'd made Ace lose his. It hadn't taken her long before he'd flipped her over to take hold of the reins.

Each time his cock drove deep inside of her, the exquisite pleasurable friction grew hotter and hotter. The coils in the gathering storm grew tauter and the pressure grew to enormous proportions.

Her muscles were so tense, too tense, and she felt as if she was about to break apart.

Ace pumped into her harder, faster and deeper, flaming the heat until she felt as if the blaze was consuming her.

The ache in her womb and pussy intensified and the internal walls grew closer and closer together. She panted heavily, trying to fill her burning lungs with air, but it was a useless endeavor.

He shoved back in deep, the head rubbing over a very sensitive spot inside of her, and when he twisted his hips, she cried out. Her body began to quake, her limbs trembling as the spiral twisted tighter and tighter.

And then she was hanging on the precipice.

Ace thrust into her twice more and she screamed. "Ace!"

Delta splintered apart into so many tiny fragments she wasn't sure she'd ever be whole again. Her whole body convulsed, quivering and quaking with a euphoric climax that stole her breath, her mind and her heart. She felt as if her very soul separated from her body and floated toward the heavens.

Juices dripped from her pussy and her mouth gaped as she screamed again.

Ace shoved a hand under her, gripped her ass and drove into her once, twice more and then stilled. He ground his pelvis into hers and groaned, the vibrations reverberating in his chest to hers as he orgasmed, spuming his cum deep into her pussy and uterus.

She didn't remember wrapping her arms around his neck and only became aware of the fact she had when she combed her fingers into the hair at the back of his neck.

Aftershocks wracked her body, causing her to moan and sigh as she tried to regain her breath. Ace's breathing was just as fast and shallow as hers. She could feel the warm moist air emitting from his mouth against her ear since he'd buried his head against her neck, and his chest rose and fell rapidly.

He nuzzled her skin with his nose, lifted his head to meet her gaze, and smiled at her. There was so much emotion in his gray eyes her breath hitched in her throat. He kissed her lightly on the lips before rolling them both to their sides. "You're amazing, darlin'."

Delta didn't think she was anything special but was glad he and his brothers seemed to think she was. They were the special ones, and even though she still had a diner to run, she was going to spend as much free time with her men as she could.

She'd already faced down death and knew life was short. Too short to work and hide away rather than living and loving.

She'd had no idea when she'd moved to Slick Rock that she would find liberation, and now that she had, she would never be imprisoned by the societal and self-imposed shackles again.

"I love you, Ace," Delta signed. She realized he didn't know what she just told him when he frowned, but it didn't bother her. He and Rocco had already learned to sign a lot, and she didn't doubt that they would be as proficient at it as she was in no time at all.

She just hoped that Major, Rocco, and Ace came to love her as much as she loved them.

Her eyelids grew heavy and drifted closed. She had no idea what time it was but didn't really care. She didn't need to go into the diner since it had been wrecked and when she woke, she would have to contact her insurance company and get an assessor out.

A whimper escaped her lips as Ace's softening cock slipped from her body, rubbing along overly sensitive tissue, and while she wanted to go to the bathroom to clean up, she just didn't have the energy. Exhaustion was pulling at her and she did nothing to stop it as she drifted into sleep.

* * * *

"She asleep?" Major asked as he and Rocco entered the room.

"Yeah," Ace answered as he stared at Delta. He couldn't seem to take his eyes off of her. He felt as if she'd reached right into his chest and was holding his heart in her delicate little hands.

"She's exhausted and no wonder." Rocco sighed as he glanced the digital clock on the bedside table. "It's after five in the morning."

"Can one of you get a cloth so I can clean her up."

"I'll get it." Rocco hurried into the bathroom.

Major had brought the clothes Delta had dropped in the living room and he put them away.

Rocco entered the room with the requested cloth in hand and he kneeled on the bed behind Delta, lifted her leg and gently wiped her clean.

"What time do you think Luke and Damon will get here?" Ace asked.

"Hopefully not before nine. She needs as much sleep as she can get." Major rubbed at the back of his neck. "We should have waited until tomorrow to make love with her."

"Why?" Rocco began stripping and then climbed in beside Delta, tugging the covers up over them.

"I feel as if we took advantage of her. She was in shock."

"She made an informed decision, bro," Ace said. "We laid everything out on the table so she wasn't going in blind."

"I know."

"Then why the guilt trip?" Rocco asked.

"I'm worried."

"That much is obvious. Spill." Ace shifted more onto his back and smiled when Delta scooted closer, snuggling into his side with her head resting on his shoulder and her leg slung over his hips. As soon as she settled, her breathing deepened and evened out again.

"I'm worried over the break in at the diner. Whoever trashed the place has it in for our woman. They knifed the booth seats and did as much damage as they could. This asshole has a vendetta and he's gunning for Delta."

"Then we don't let her out of our sight," Ace stated calmly.

"That's a given, but how the hell are we going to find this fucker if we don't know who we're looking for?" Major asked.

"He'll slip up eventually," Rocco began, "and when he does we'll be waiting to take him down."

"Are you going to sleep in here, too?" Ace asked.

Major shook his head. "No. I'll have my turn tomorrow night."

"He's worried," Ace murmured.

"And you're not?" Rocco asked.

"Yes, but Delta's not stupid. She texted me as soon as she realized someone had broken in."

"Thank fuck." Rocco brushed a strand of hair from Delta's cheek. "But what if she doesn't realize she's in trouble until it's too late?"

"That's why we can't let her out of our sight." Ace flicked the lamp off and held onto Delta. He as just as concerned as his brothers, but he'd been trying to lighten the tension thickening the air.

Major and Rocco were more serious and domineering than Ace, and while he could be just like his brothers, he tried to keep an optimistic outlook so they wouldn't go all He-Man on Delta. If they began giving her orders regarding the diner, he knew she was going to be pissed. Nonetheless, one them was going to be with her at all times, or as much as they could. He knew sometimes circumstances changed, especially if there was an emergency of some sort.

He and his brothers were volunteer fire fighters, and since it had been a long, hot, dry summer, the conditions were prime for a bush fire. A shiver of trepidation raced up his spine.

Ace had wished and prayed for a good downpour or two just like everyone else in the county, but his prayers hadn't been answered. It was so dry they'd had to start carting water in just like all the other farmers in the community.

He pushed his disconcerting thoughts aside and breathed in Delta's scent.

He and his brothers had finally found their woman. He should be thinking happy thoughts and not letting his brothers' pessimism get to him.

Chapter Fourteen

As soon as she surfaced from sleep, Delta knew she wasn't alone. She was surrounded in heat and sandwiched between two large, muscular, manly bodies. She forced her eyes open and blinked to clear the sleep haze from her vision and stretched. Her stiff muscles and sore pussy reminded her of the amazing night she'd had making love with Major, Rocco, and Ace, but that also had her remembering that her dream business was on hold.

She sat up with a gasp when she realized she hadn't notified any of her staff not to bother coming to work, and while she didn't have much money, she was going to pay them what they'd normally earn whilst working for her. She just hoped that her insurance company would cover all the costs, including her staff's wages, but if they didn't, she would continue to pay them out of her own pocket.

When she caught movement on both sides of her she glanced at Rocco and then Ace. They sat up beside her and were frowning in concern.

"What's wrong, honey?" Rocco asked.

She glanced toward the doorway when Major entered the room and met his gaze so he could explain her concerns to the other men. "I haven't texted Cindy and the other women."

Delta scrambled to her hands and knees and crawled down toward the end of the bed. Once she gained her feet she glanced around for her cell phone, not remembering where she'd left it.

Major came closer and wrapped his arms around her waist. He kissed her lightly on the lips and then drew back so he could sign to her. "It's still early yet, baby. You have time to notify your staff. If you want, I can do it for you using your cell phone, while you take a shower. The sheriffs are coming over to take your statement this morning."

"What time is it?" she asked.

"It's just before seven. What time do the other women turn up?"

"Seven-thirty, but Enya was going to make some muffins, cakes, and pies. She's probably already been up for hours to make all those things."

"The food won't go to waste, Delta." Major guided her toward the bathroom. "The men working to fix up the diner will no doubt devour everything in sight."

"But I need…what men?"

"Get cleaned up. When you come out to the kitchen we'll explain everything."

She gnawed on her lip and nodded. Usually she needed at least one cup of coffee in her to kick start her brain, but two cups were preferable. Delta frowned as she entered the bathroom, a little worried that the men were trying to take her over. If that was the case she was going to have to put her foot down. Just because she was hearing impaired didn't mean she didn't have a brain and couldn't do things for herself.

She hurried through her shower and once she was dressed, put her still damp hair up in a braid and brushed her teeth. After a cursory glance in the mirror at her jean shorts and sleeveless shirt, she headed out to the kitchen. Even though it was still early morning, the summer heat was already climbing the temperature scale, and while she loved the bright sunny days and the blue sky, Delta didn't deal well with soaring temperatures. The only reason she'd been able to cope cooking in the hot kitchen of the diner was because she had air-conditioning. Last night she'd been too caught up in Major, Rocco, and Ace to notice if they had cooling in their house, but she suspected they did since she hadn't been sweating up a storm. Well at least not while making love to them anyway.

When she saw the two sheriffs already sitting at the dining table with mugs of coffee she paused in the doorway and took a deep breath. This was one of the times she wished she could speak and hear so she could relate what happened at the diner verbally, but she was lucky that Major and Luke were able to sign. Of course, Rocco, Ace, and even Damon were learning and that made her heart feel warm and fuzzy. No one had ever gone out of their way to learn the skill of sign language just for her. Having all of these men do something like that just so they could communicate with her was amazing.

She glanced toward Ace when he began to walk toward her. He smiled, winked, and enfolded her hand in his before leading her to the dining table. After she was seated, he sat in the chair next to her. Major sat on her other side, placing a steaming cup of coffee in front of her. He cupped her cheek in his big, warm hand. "Are you hungry, baby?"

Delta shook her head. "No." She was too nervous to be hungry. Her stomach was full of nervous butterflies. She turned her gaze toward Luke when he tapped the table to get her attention.

"Can you tell me what happened last night, Delta?" Luke asked.

She nodded, took a sip of coffee, and then started to explain.

When she'd finished, Luke asked, "What made you wake up?"

Heat crept into her cheeks. She didn't want to tell the men she had nightmares, but she wasn't going to lie to the sheriff. "I had a bad dream." Delta lowered her gaze when she saw sympathy in Luke's eyes. He knew all about her being shot in her previous job. The first time he'd come to the diner he'd entered the kitchen to introduce himself. He'd virtually interrogated her until she'd spilt her guts to him. He'd apologized for giving her the third degree, but then he'd explained it was his and his men's job to make sure no one with bad intentions was allowed to reside in their town. He'd also been the one to tell the previous diner owner that it was okay for Delta to buy the place. At first she'd been appalled with the amount of control the law had in Slick Rock, but Luke had also gone on to explain that it was his job to keep everyone safe and he couldn't do that if he was kept in the dark.

Rocco leaned around Ace and asked, "Do you have nightmares often?"

She swallowed around the lump in her throat and nodded.

"You have nothing to be ashamed of, honey," Rocco said. "We have PTSD, too. Working the land has helped lessen the effects fighting in wars had on us. Since we know what you're going through we can help you."

Delta sighed with relief, nodded and smiled with appreciation. Major, Rocco, and Ace were so caring, it brought tears to her eyes. In fact, all the men she'd seen that were involved in the unusual relationships seemed to be the same way. She turned to meet Major's gaze after getting her emotions back under control. "Did you contact my employees?"

"I did." Major nodded. "Enya is going to take all the food she's made down for the clean-up and construction crew."

"Did you organize that?" She frowned.

"No. Giles Alcott did. He and his brothers are going to cover the cost of fixing the diner up."

Delta shoved to her feet and started pacing. She didn't understand why men she'd never met would do such a thing and wondered why they were. Were they doing this so she would be beholden to them? Or was it for another reason? Did they think she was incapable of contacting her insurance company? She was sick and tired of people treating her as if she was an idiot instead of being hearing impaired.

She spun back around and gasped when she slammed up against a big, hard body. Rocco grasped her upper arms to steady her. "Calm down, honey. You're working yourself up for no reason."

She dislodged his hold on her arms. "Am I?"

Delta waved her hands in the air in agitation. "You all must think I'm useless." Tears burned her eyes but she refused to let them fall. She spun away and stalked into the kitchen, grabbed a clean cup from the cupboard, and poured herself another cup of coffee from the pot. She didn't want to be near them right now, so she ignored the fact she already had half a cup of coffee sitting on the dining room table. She took a big gulp from the mug, relishing the burn of the hot bitter brew as it slid down her throat. Even though she was aware of movement behind her she kept her back toward the men, ignoring them. She felt hurt beyond belief and wished she could yell at them for thinking so little of her, just like everyone else she'd met in her life.

Why did people always seem to think she was mentally and physically impaired as well as deaf? She had two arms and legs, and a brain. She was as capable as any other normal person.

She tensed when hands clasped her shoulders and while she tried to resist when those strong hands turned her around, she wasn't strong enough. She didn't need to look up to know it was Major holding onto her. His scent had filled her nose as soon as he came up behind her. He clasped her chin between his finger and thumb and tilted her gaze up to his.

"We know damn well you aren't useless, Delta," Major signed as well as spoke angrily. She could tell he was pissed because he was moving jerkily. "Why the hell would you even say that?"

She stepped back out of his hold, her lower back bumping into the counter edge but she ignored the slight pain. "You and your brothers are taking over. You contacted my staff. One of you organized for the security company to fix up the damage at the diner. I have insurance. I was going to contact the company this morning, but you didn't give me the chance."

"Come and sit back down." Major held his hand out to her.

She eyed his large, callused palm and although she wanted to be petty and ignore his peace offering, she wasn't like that. She needed to hear him and his brothers out as well as explain how she needed to control her own life. Delta had a feeling if she gave them an inch, they would take a whole damn mile. She couldn't let that happen. With a sigh, she placed her hand in his and let him guide her back to the dining table. She was glad to see that Luke and Damon didn't seem to be paying them any attention and were talking to each other.

Instead of helping her back into her previous seat, Major sat down, snagged an arm around her waist and tugged her onto his lap. She crossed her arms over her chest and glared at him.

"First of all, we are not trying to take over, baby. When I offered to contact your staff, you could have said no. I was just trying to be helpful. Secondly, we didn't arrange for Giles to get the workmen to fix up the diner. That was his idea. He called late last night to apologize. He had a new guy working the monitors who either didn't give a shit about doing his job or was just plain incompetent. The security guy should have picked up that that the power had been cut to the building and called the police right away. If he'd done that, you wouldn't have been in danger and there would be no need for the construction workers. Giles decided to foot the bill as an apology to you. He's trying to make amends."

Guilt at her outburst assaulted her heart. Delta was so used to people thinking she was an idiot, she'd automatically jumped to conclusions. The hurt and anger faded. "I'm sorry. I'm just so used to people treating me like I'm an imbecile, I overreacted."

"You don't have to apologize, baby."

"Yes, I do."

Rocco took her hand in his, lifted it to his mouth and kissed the back of it. He winked at her and then said, "We like that you have fire in you, honey. You'll keep us on our toes."

Delta blinked and then nodded. She'd expected them to be pissed at her after her outburst. Other people would have been, but not her men. She glanced over at Ace to see him leaning back in his chair with his hands locked behind his head and a big grin on his face.

She realized then that she would never understand how the male psyche worked.

"We ran the prints," Luke said.

Delta tensed, hoping that the sheriffs knew who'd broken in and trashed the diner.

"We don't have anything to go on," Luke continued. "We were only able to get partial prints and nothing came up on the data base."

Damon leaned his elbows on the table. "Do you know who'd want to hurt you, Delta?"

"No." She sighed. "I've only met a few people and they've all been women."

"That doesn't mean anything," Luke said. "Women can be just as dangerous as men. Even though you weren't attacked, thank the Lord, this was personal. Someone is real pissed with you."

"What about when you were in Chicago?" Damon asked. "Did you leave an ex-boyfriend or a disgruntled customer behind?"

"I didn't date," Delta answered. "I only ever interacted with people when I was working at the bank."

"Did you upset a fellow employee?" Luke asked.

She shook her head and then lowered her gaze when heated embarrassment suffused her cheeks. After sucking in a deep breath, she met Luke's gaze again. "No. None of the employees ever gave me a second glance."

"That leaves the customers." Damon frowned. "Or maybe the bank manager?"

"The manager may have been an ass but I don't think he would bother to follow me here."

"You can't know that for sure, baby," Major said.

"Actually, I do. He didn't want to employ me at all, but apparently the board of directors told him to."

"That could be reason enough for motive." Ace crossed his arms over his chest.

"I can't see it. The smarmy weasel had me segregated from the other employees. The only time I ever interacted with anyone was when I was serving the customers."

"Can you remember their names, honey?" Rocco asked.

Delta nodded. "Most of my customers were physically impaired in some way, too."

"I'll need you to write their names down on a list for me, Delta."

"Okay." She sighed. She would do as Luke asked, but she had a feeling he was barking up the wrong tree.

If she hadn't been so exhausted, so replete after making love with her men, she would have stayed up all night trying to work out who had a grudge against her, but she had a feeling she wouldn't know unless she came face to face with the bastard. She'd never done anything to deliberately hurt anyone else or to treat anyone differently than she'd wanted to be treated herself. She knew what it was like to be looked at as if she had two heads.

Luke and Damon rose and headed toward the entrance. Ace and Rocco followed the men from the kitchen to see them out.

Delta sighed tiredly and leaned against Major. All she wanted to do was head back to bed and fall into a deep sleep, but she needed to head to the diner to make sure everything was being fixed the way she wanted it. She also needed to give Enya the money she would have spent for the baking she'd done. After that she wanted to go over the books and then maybe she'd find time to write the list the sheriff wanted.

She needed to contact her lawyer to write up a partnership contract for Enya and Lilac as well. After everything was done, she would need to rewrite the employee schedule, and maybe she would give herself a day off every once in a while. Although the diner was still her dream and passion, she was tired, and after thinking things through, she wanted to share her business with the other two women. Every time she met those women's gazes, she saw sadness and vulnerability in their eyes. She might not know what they'd been through or what was haunting them, but she liked them a lot and wanted to keep them around. She wasn't trying to buy their friendship, even though it may have seemed that way. What she was trying to do was help them out in the only way she could. She had a terrible feeling they'd endured more than she ever had. This was her way of being a friend and helping them out at the same time. They'd already proven to her they were trustworthy, fantastic chefs, and she wanted to deepen the friendship that was already forming between them.

She'd never imagined wanting to do anything but cook after making the decision to follow her passion, but Major, Rocco, and Ace had made her rethink things. Although she still wanted to cook and run the diner, her priorities had changed. If she continued working the long hours she had been, her relationship with the Porter men would be doomed before it really got off the ground. No relationship, new or otherwise, survived without putting any time or effort into it. She wanted to be able to spend more time with her men and she wouldn't be able to do that if she had no spare time.

Delta just hoped that Enya and Lilac didn't refuse the partnership offer, because she wasn't certain she had the energy to keep going the way she had been.

She wasn't sure what she'd do if the other women refused her offer. No, that wasn't true. Delta would just face every day like she usually did.

* * * *

Major hoped that Delta wasn't still hurt and angry with him and his brothers, and while she'd apologized for her outburst, he thought she might still be upset with them. Every time she breathed out she was sighing loudly as if she had the weight of the world upon her shoulders.

He grasped hold of her braid and pulled gently until her gaze lifted to his. "Are you okay, baby? You're not still pissed at us, are you?"

"No," she replied. "I'm sorry I went off on a tangent."

Major stroked a finger down her cheek. He loved how soft her skin was against his flesh and knew he would never get enough or ever get sick of touching her. "Stop saying sorry, Delta. You're allowed to be human, just like the rest of us. Now, why are you frowning?"

"I've just been thinking about all the things I need to do."

"Like what?"

"Well, I want to go down to the diner and make sure the contractors are fixing things up the same as they were."

"You don't need to worry about that, baby. Giles, Remy, or Brandt will make sure of it."

She sat up a little straighter and Major had to bite the inside of his cheek to stop the moan bubbling up in his chest from escaping. Even though he and his brothers had made love to her, she was still such an innocent. Delta seemed to be totally oblivious to the fact that her sexy ass was rubbing against his cock and every time she moved, he was getting harder and harder.

"I don't know those men though."

"Do you trust me, baby?" he asked and held his breath while awaiting an answer. Air exploded from his lungs when she nodded and the tension he didn't know he was holding in his muscles dissipated.

"I do. Trust you that is."

"That's good, because I can tell you now that Giles and his brothers will make sure all the work is top-notch. You don't have to worry about the construction workers cutting corners. Okay?"

"Okay, but I still need to go."

"Why?" Major couldn't help himself. He'd been eying her braid and while he loved her hair, he hated the way she'd tied it up. He loved seeing her long blonde hair falling down around her face, past her shoulders with the ends swishing at her hips. He tugged the tie from the ends and threaded his fingers through her hair until it was falling down her back.

"Hey, what are you doing?"

"Looking at your hair. I love how thick, shiny and soft it is. And there's so damn much of it."

When she harrumphed and glared at him, Major couldn't help but smile. She was so fucking cute and sexy. "Do you know how long it takes to put up?"

"You should wear it down all the time."

"I can't. I need to have it up when I'm working around food. Can you imagine how mortified I'd be if someone found some of my hair in their dinner?"

"I hadn't thought of that." He combed his finger through the silky mass and then massaged her skull lightly. When she moaned and closed her eyes, he nearly came in his pants. She was so fucking sensual and didn't have a clue how she affected him or his brothers. Jealousy pierced his heart as he envisaged other single men staring at her beautiful hair and gorgeous body. He had a change of heart and decided she could, should, wear her hair up, whenever he and his brothers weren't around to protect her. When he realized he was being an ass, even if he hadn't voiced his thoughts out loud, he brought his mind back on track.

"Why do you still need to go to the diner?"

"I have some paperwork to catch up on and I need to go through the kitchen to see what if any of the supplies were ruined."

He hated to tell her but she needed to know so she could reorder ingredients for when the diner was ready to reopen. He leaned his forehead against hers and then kissed her softly on the lips. "You're going to need to buy everything, baby."

"Everything?" she asked and lowered her eyelids.

His heart clenched when a tear leaked from the corner of both of her eyes and he wrapped his arms around her when she pressed her face against his neck. He was still holding her close when Ace and Rocco came back.

"What's going on?" Rocco asked as he rushed toward Delta.

"Is she all right?"

"Yeah. I just told her she needed to replace all her kitchen ingredients."

Delta sat up when he started talking and gazed at Ace and Rocco.

Rocco crouched down in front of her and cupped her face in his hands. "Everything will be okay, honey. We'll help you get all the supplies you need and want."

"No, I'll put in an insurance claim. I'll get Luke to email the damage report to the company." She met Major's gaze again. "Can you get this Giles person to put in writing that his company is covering the repair costs?"

"Sure, baby. Why don't we all go to the diner? That way we can introduce you to Giles and/or his brothers and you can ask him yourself."

"Don't you have chores you need to do here?"

"You're more important, Delta."

"But this ranch is your livelihood, you can't just ignore it."

"We aren't ignoring it, baby. I was up before daybreak mucking out the barn and making sure the cattle had plenty of feed and water. Ace and Rocco can pick up the slack when we get back," he said firmly.

Delta sighed and nodded. "I just need to redo my hair and then we can go."

Major watched her sexy ass swaying back and forth as she hurried away.

"Do you think this is a good idea?" Ace asked.

"We can't stop her from working, Ace."

"I know. That's not what I meant. I'm just worried that seeing the diner in such disrepair will break her."

"Our woman is a lot stronger than she looks," Rocco said. "She's had to deal with a lot in her life and from what I can tell, she hasn't let other people's prejudices or actions hold her back."

"Yeah, okay. You're right." Ace scrubbed a hand over his face. "We need to talk to her about those nightmares."

"Yes, we do," Major agreed. "But we'll leave that for later. Right now, we need to help her with whatever she wants done. Delta isn't used to having help. She's never been able to lean on someone when she needed to. We have to show her that she can rely on us to back her up when she requires it."

"You don't think she trusts us?" Ace snapped.

"No, that's not what I mean. She trusts us, bro. She would never have agreed to make love with us or try a relationship if she didn't." Major shoved to his feet, gathered the used coffee mugs and took them to the kitchen. He rinsed them and put them in the dishwasher.

"What we need is for her to talk to us more," Rocco said. "She's been on her own for so long, she's never had to answer to anyone. That didn't come out right. Delta's intelligent and she thinks a lot without voicing what she's thinking. We want her to be able to bounce ideas off of us. We want her to be able to come to one or all of us if we she has a problem, and while she's trusted us with her body and she knows we'll never intentionally do anything to hurt her, we need her to trust us with her heart. We start earning her respect and trust by helping her out where we can, and hopefully, the rest will follow."

Major was surprised that Rocco was able to voice his thoughts better than he was. Ace, although, a little impatient, was usually the one to be able to tap into a female's psyche better than he and Rocco could. Although his younger brother was no expert on the opposite sex either, he was usually more in tune to their emotions.

"What he said." Major pointed at Rocco and then turned toward the doorway when he heard Delta returning.

Major just hoped that seeing the diner didn't bring her to tears. He was already furious at the fucker for scaring her. It would tear his heart out if he saw her crying again.

Chapter Fifteen

Leo couldn't believe that Woodall Construction Company had been called in to fix up the diner he'd wrecked. While he couldn't show it, inside he was laughing with glee. He'd been directed to remove the booth seats which were going to be replaced. The other guys were pulling up the linoleum floor since he'd ruined it by slashing it with his knife.

He'd made sure to keep his expression blank so as not to give himself away, but when the two sheriffs had shown up, he'd started sweating up a storm. When they'd first walked through the door, he'd thought the law had been there for him. He hadn't been able to breathe until they began talking with the Woodall brothers. When they disappeared into the kitchen he sighed with relief. The only way he was going to get through the day was to go about his work as he normally did and pretend that nothing had happened.

Leo had been watching the sheriffs and the deputies since the moment he'd hit town and knew they weren't stupid men. There was a rumor about that the sheriffs always checked out anybody new to town, but so far he'd been lucky. Maybe he'd be able to keep flying under the radar since he was working for Trent and Tristan Woodall. The sheriffs might think that the Woodall brothers had checked him out before they hired him on.

He chuckled to himself. The assholes wouldn't find anything anyway. While he'd been searching for the deaf cunt, he'd changed his name. The surname he was using was his mother's maiden name. Unless they went looking deeper, the sheriffs and the brothers would never even know he was related to the man who'd died in that bank in Chicago.

Just as he was lining up the new booth seats so he could secure them to the floor the deaf bitch entered with three other men. He lowered his head hoping his cap would keep his face in the shadows as he watched her look about. She was tense and looked as if she was about to cry.

You deserve everything coming your way, you cunt. You'll be begging me to kill you by the time I've finished with you.

* * * *

Delta sucked in a deep breath as she Rocco helped her out of the truck. While she couldn't believe how much work the construction crew had gotten through already, seeing the diner brought back the fear she'd faced last night. She couldn't stop the shiver racing up her spine and making her body quake. She was glad that she had Ace, Rocco, and Major with her.

Rocco slung an arm around her shoulders and tucked her in under his arm. Although the temperature was already up in the mid to high eighties, she felt cold to the bone and had goosebumps on her skin.

"You okay, honey?" Rocco asked.

She nodded, savoring the heat emanating from his body as she gazed into his eyes.

"You don't have to do this if you don't want to."

"Yes, I do."

"Let me, Ace, or Major know if it gets too much. Okay?"

"Okay."

She leaned on him as they walked toward the entrance. All the windows had been replaced. The slashed booth seats had been removed and the men were pulling up the linoleum floor. As she walked in the door she saw that Luke and Damon were talking to a man she'd never met and from the tenseness around his jaw and lips, she guessed that he was Giles or one of his brothers.

There was a lot of drilling and hammering going on but thankfully, she couldn't hear any of it. Luke nodded and smiled at her and pointed toward the hallway with a quirked eyebrow.

She nodded and followed the men. When she got to the kitchen doorway, she covered her mouth in shock. There were a few men picking up smashed crockery and dumping it into the trash, but seeing all the food strewn about the floor had tears welling in her eyes. There was flour and sugar everywhere. Bags of coffee beans had been slashed open and were spilling out onto the floor. There were packets of meat tossed about and the fresh herbs she had growing in pots looked as if they'd been ground under a heel.

Delta almost jumped out of her skin when a hand caressed up and down her arm. She met Rocco's concerned gaze and while she tried to hold back the sob in her chest, she failed.

Rocco tugged her into his arms and held her tight. She wrapped her arms around his waist, pressed her forehead to his chest and hugged him back as she tried to get her emotions under control. She wiped her damp cheeks on his T-shirt, drew in a deep ragged breath and drew back.

"We'll help you get what you need, honey."

Delta nodded and then headed to her office. There was so much to do but she was determined to have everything ready to open the diner again as fast as possible. She wasn't about to let some asshole ruin her dreams. With a determined set of her jaw she went straight to her computer as soon as she entered her office.

There was no time for her to wallow over something that was out of her control. She would put every ounce of her energy into setting things right. She couldn't afford to lose the plot now, not when she had staff relying on her for work. She might not be able to hear but she'd seen the shadows in Enya's and Lilac's gazes and knew they dealt with something terrible just as she had. While she didn't know the women well, she wasn't about to let things slide. Those women needed to work to survive just like most people did, but Delta had a feeling they needed companionship just as much as she did, even if she hadn't realized it. They needed a place to belong and Slick Rock was that place in her eyes, her heart. Hopefully, Enya and Lilac would realize that, too.

Delta pushed her introspection aside and glanced about the room from behind her desk. All the men had been talking earnestly and instead of trying to read their lips to figure out what was going on, she'd been lost in her own little world.

She met Major's gaze when he took a step toward her and waited for him to introduce her to the other man.

"Delta, this is Giles Alcott, baby. He and his brothers run the security company in town."

"Nice to meet you, Giles."

Giles smiled at her and then gazed at Major before turning back to look at her again. "It's nice to meet you, too, Delta. I want to apologize for the incompetence of my most recent employee."

"None of this is your fault. If you want to blame someone, blame the person who broke into the diner and destroyed it. But thank you for the apology and for getting started on fixing the diner up so quickly." Delta could tell Giles still carried the guilt over what had happened, however there was nothing she could do about what he was feeling, even if he nodded as if agreeing with her.

"Everything should be finished by tomorrow night and you'll be able to reopen for business again, the day after," Giles said.

Delta gaped at him. She hadn't expected things to be finished so quickly. "Wow, that's fast. Thank you. Thanks so much."

Giles smiled. "You're welcome. If you ever need anything, don't hesitate to get in contact with me or my brothers. And I promise you, nothing like this will ever happen again."

Delta nodded and then waved when he waved at her just before he left the office. She had no doubt that he was going to personally inspect the security system himself.

"Do you need help with anything?" Major asked.

She gazed at her computer and shook her head. She was going to be sitting at her desk for hours placing orders, taking care of the paper work, and she'd emailed a lawyer to meet her just after lunch. She couldn't see herself finishing the tasks she'd set herself before late afternoon.

"No thanks. I'm going to be here all day. Why don't you all head on back to the ranch? I know you have chores that need to be done."

"You and Ace go," Rocco said. "I'll hang around here."

"You don't need—"

Rocco slashed his hand through the air and gazed at her determinedly. "There is every need, honey. I'm not about to let you out of my sight until the sheriffs catch this bastard."

"So you're going to follow me around everywhere? You're going to be bored out of your mind."

"I don't care about being bored, Delta. All I care about is keeping you safe, just as Major and Ace do."

Delta's heart swelled with emotion. They were so caring and loving. How could she not love Major, Rocco, and Ace back?

She stood and moved away from her desk as Major walked toward her. He wrapped his arms around her waist and pulled her tight against his body. She wrapped her arms around his waist and hugged him back. He drew away, leaned down and kissed her long, hard and deep. By the time he let her up for air, she was wet and panting. He tapped her on the nose, kissed her lightly on the forehead and released her. "Stay out of trouble, baby."

She nodded and when he turned away from her she gazed at his muscular ass encased in his blue denim jeans and licked her lips. When Ace moved to stand in front of her, she lifted her gaze to his.

He was grinning because he'd obviously caught her staring at his brother's butt.

"Don't go wandering off by yourself. Okay darlin'?" Ace asked, but she could tell by the determined set of his jaw that is question had really been an order.

"I won't."

"Good. You need to stay safe, Delta. I don't know what I'd do if something happened to you."

Her heart flipped in her chest and she was about to tell him she loved him, but he slanted his mouth over hers before she could and then she was lost in his kisses and his taste.

When he released her mouth, she was a shivering mass of need, but this wasn't the time or place to give into temptation. Maybe tonight she would find the courage to tell the three men how much she loved them.

* * * *

Rocco sat on the sofa across from the desk and watched Delta work. She was so engrossed in what she was doing she didn't even seem to realize she was gnawing on her lip. He wanted to get up and close and lock the door so he could make love with her, but there was no way in hell he was going to give into his urges. There was no way he wanted the men working about the place to hear the sexy noises she made when she came.

He glanced at his watch and was surprised to see it was just after lunch time. He'd been so mesmerized by his woman, he hadn't realized how fast the time was flying by. When he caught movement from the corner of his eye near the door way, he surged to his feet and hurried across the room, blocking the stranger from entering with his body.

"Who the hell are you?"

"Um, I'm Vincent Maloney. I'm a lawyer. Ms. Sykes requested a meeting with me."

"About what?"

He shifted his weight to the side when he felt Delta behind him, blocking her view of the suited man. He wasn't about to let anyone into her office until he was sure he wasn't about to hurt his woman.

"She's asked me to draw up a contract for a partnership with two of her employees."

Rocco relaxed and stepped aside. He wasn't surprised by their woman's generosity, but he wondered why she hadn't told him and his brothers about her plans.

Delta shook the lawyers hand and indicated for him to sit in the seat across from her desk. Rocco moved to stand behind her and to the side. He needed to see everything that was going on so his woman wasn't duped in any way.

She glanced up at him over her shoulder and he had to bite back a smile when she rolled her eyes at him. When she turned back to face the lawyer, she picked up a pad of paper and began to ask questions.

Vincent didn't seem to think the way they were communicating was odd, so Rocco figured she must have already told her lawyer she was hearing impaired. Rocco read all of her questions and Maloney's answers and leaned back against the wall when he was satisfied with the results. The suit wasn't trying to gyp Delta at all. He was definitely on the up and up.

Once the lawyer had departed, Rocco couldn't keep his distance a moment longer. He bent down scooped her up from the chair and sat with her in his lap. She met his gaze and then she leaned in and kissed him. He kissed her back, passionately, twining his tongue with hers before gliding together as they devoured each other with wild carnality. He broke the kiss when he heard her stomach growl and cursed at himself for not taking better care of her.

"Was there any food that was able to be salvaged in the kitchen?" Rocco asked after getting his breath back.

She shook her head.

"Let me call the hotel to send something over."

"I can wait till we get home."

His heart surged with warmth and hope. Delta already thought about the ranch as home. That was a very good thing. He and his brothers had planned to talk to her tonight and ask her to move in with them, hoping they weren't moving too fast, or too soon.

"Are you done for the day?" Rocco asked.

"Almost." She pressed her forehead to his and then kissed him lightly, lovingly on the lips. "I'm just waiting for a confirmation email from the suppliers."

Rocco stood, taking her with him and after kissing her again, he deposited her back in her seat. "I'm just going to check out front. Don't you move from this office. All right?"

"I won't."

He nodded and headed out pulling his cell phone from his pocket to call Major to come and pick them up. He was going to order take out from the hotel. Delta was a stubborn little thing and would never admit how tired she was, but she didn't need to. He'd have to be blind not to see the dark smudges of exhaustion marring her soft creamy skin.

He and his brothers should let her sleep after she'd eaten, but they were selfish bastards when they came to Delta. They had plans to make love to her together. The yearning to claim her as one was too strong to ignore.

Other people would probably think and call them primitive but he didn't give a shit. He and his brothers wouldn't feel as if she was theirs until they'd taken her all at the same time.

If that made them Neanderthals or throwbacks to the caveman era, so be it.

He'd never cared what other people thought of him before and wasn't about to start now. As long as Delta was on board with what they wanted, it was no one else's business what they did in their home and in the bedroom but their own.

"Rocco," Major answered on the first ring.

He'd never admit it, but big brother was just as eager if not more so to get the ball rolling on claiming Delta for all time. Usually Major was the most patient out of all of them but Rocco suspected he'd been watching the clock all day long. He couldn't keep the smile out of his voice when he said, "Come and get us."

"We're on our way."

"Stop by the hotel before heading to the diner. I'm going to order some take out. She's exhausted."

Major sighed. "Maybe we should let her sleep after she's eaten."

"Let's see how things play out," he suggested. "She called the ranch home."

"She did?"

Rocco couldn't miss the excitement in his brother's voice. His heart flipped and butterflies started fluttering in his belly. "She did."

"That's fucking great."

"It is."

"Do you think we should leave talking about her nightmares for another time?" Major asked uncertainly.

Rocco had never heard or seen his brother indecisive about anything, but since they were playing for keeps none of them wanted to fuck up. Delta was the most important person in their world. He wasn't sure what he'd do if they lost her before they truly had her.

Chapter Sixteen

As soon as the confirmation email came in, Delta shut the computer down and began to gather up her paperwork to file in the cabinet. She'd just turned toward her desk to grab her bag when she saw one of the workmen replacing the damaged door to the above stairs apartment.

When he turned to the side and bent to pick up the new lock, she frowned. He looked familiar but she couldn't remember ever seeing him before. She tried to see his face, which was hidden in shadows under the cap he was wearing, but he turned away and began to fix a new lock to the door.

She sighed tiredly and pushed him from her thoughts. She couldn't wait to get back to the ranch. After she'd eaten she was going to soak in the big spa bath and wash the long day away.

She was excited about offering Lilac and Enya a partnership and hoped they agreed to come on board. Although she hadn't seen Enya, Major had told her the men had been raving over how delicious the other woman's muffins, cakes, and pies were.

Delta was excited about sharing her business with them because she had a feeling they were going to be a resounding success. How could they not when there would be three chefs working behind the scenes to feed the people of Slick Rock? She was the least experienced of them all, but since the locals had filled the seats, she figured her food couldn't be too terrible.

She exited the office, closed and locked the door and started down the hallway just as Rocco was coming toward her. When she saw the scowl on his face, she guessed he wasn't happy about something. He glared at her and she sighed when she realized he was unhappy with her.

"What?" she asked as she stopped a few feet in front of him.

"Why didn't you wait for me?"

"There's no danger, Rocco," she replied. "The place is swarming with men. If I'd been in danger all I had to do was scream."

Rocco glanced over her shoulder, threaded his fingers with hers, and guided her toward the exit. Once they were outside he turned to face her again and clasped both her hands.

"And what would you have done if someone had come up from behind you, placed his hand over your mouth and dragged you out the back?"

A shiver of apprehension raced up her spine. She hadn't even thought about that, and unless she was alert to her surroundings she might never know if someone was behind her. She tugged to pull her hands out of his, but he held fast.

"I didn't even think about it." She sucked in a deep breath. "I'm sorry."

Rocco pulled her into his arms and hugged her, glancing about to make sure no one was watching them. When he saw the coast was clear, he backed her up against the brick wall and pressed his body into hers. "Promise me you won't take those kinds of chances again."

"I promise," she answered immediately. "I'm not going to purposely put myself in danger, Rocco, but I'm also not used to thinking about every little thing I do."

"You have to start, honey. Thinking, that is. We don't want you left alone until the sheriffs have this asshole behind bars. I couldn't take it if something happened to you, Delta. It would rip my heart to shreds if you got hurt. Don't you know how fucking much I love you?"

She gaped at him before snapping her mouth closed. She'd never expected to hear those words on a man's lips in regard to her. Love and happiness filled her heart to overflowing and she couldn't contain the tears burning the back of her eyes. She hadn't noticed she'd closed her eyes until she felt him move restlessly. His muscles were bunched with tension and she felt terrible for not reacting sooner. She opened her eyes, sucked in a breath, and cupped his cheeks between her hands.

"I love you, too, Rocco."

She didn't get to say anything else because he slammed his mouth over hers and kissed her voraciously. She sank into him, savoring his touch, his manly flavor on her tongue, all the while tears of joy rolled down her cheeks.

Rocco slowed the kiss, nipping and licking at her lips until he finally lifted his mouth from hers. Her breath caught in her throat when she saw his love for her in his gaze. Her heart slammed against her sternum when she realized that Major and Ace looked at her the same way. How could she have been so blind? Because she'd lost one of her senses, she was usually quick to pick up on others, but where the Porter men were concerned she'd been totally oblivious.

It took her a few moments to realize that she been too scared to even acknowledge what she'd seen in their gazes. Everything had happened fast. Way too fast and she hadn't trusted them or herself. She'd honestly thought she'd been very open with them. Delta hadn't spoken to anyone as much as she had Rocco, Ace, and Major, but she'd held part of herself back. She'd still been expecting a verbal slap down or to be physically shunned because she was different. She'd thought that the Porter men had liberated her from bias and while they had, she'd still had partial shackles tethering her to her cynical expectations.

Rocco smoothed his thumbs over her cheeks, wiping the moisture away. When he glanced over his shoulder, she tilted her head to the side to see Major and Ace pulling up into a parking space. As soon as the truck stopped both men were out of the vehicle and racing toward them.

"What's wrong?" Major frowned as he glanced about. "Did something happen?"

"No," she answered.

Rocco nodded and smiled. "We'll talk when we get home. Did you pick up the take-out?"

"We did," Ace replied just before he shoved Rocco away from her. He slung an arm around her shoulders and guided her toward the truck.

"That wasn't very nice," she told him.

Ace didn't seem to care. He grinned and winked at her before saying, "He's had you to himself all, day, darlin'. It's my turn now."

Delta giggled. She'd loved this playful side of Ace and hoped to see far more of it. In fact, she hoped all her men began to play and laugh more. They were all so serious all the time, but then she had been, too. Delta decided it was high time to have some fun in their lives, but she wasn't sure what to do or how to make that happen. Maybe she could ask one of the other women to suggest something.

She sighed as she slid across the back seat after Ace lifted her into the truck, giving him room to get in, too. She was about to move to the opposite side but Ace clasped her wrist to stop her.

"Stay next to me, darlin'." Ace reached behind her and tugged the safety belt down and over her before securing it in place. He looped his arm across her shoulders and she snuggled into his side as she rested her head on his arm. Her eyelids grew heavy as Major backed the truck out of the parking space, and while she was so hungry she could feel her empty belly gurgling, she wasn't sure she'd be able to stay awake for the ride home let alone to eat.

Ace stroked a finger down her cheek and she couldn't stop herself from nuzzling into his palm. "What did you do today, darlin'?"

She'd never had anyone asked her that question before, and while it was foreign it was also heart-warming. She signed slowly as she told him about her day and then waited for the question she could see in his gaze.

"Did you say you had a lawyer show up? And he drew up contracts for you? What the hell for?"

"Don't go getting your shorts in a twist, Ace," Rocco said as he signed for her benefit. The poor man looked uncomfortable since he was twisted in an awkward position so she could see him speaking. She covered her mouth to stop the laugh forming in her chest from escaping her mouth when she saw the disgruntled look Ace gave Rocco, but it was a losing battle. Laughter burst from her parted lips. Rocco was smiling at her, and when she gazed at Ace she found him smiling, too. Major gazed at her from the rearview mirror and from the crinkles she could see at the corner of his eyes, he was also smiling.

Delta had no idea why she was laughing. Rocco's statement hadn't been that funny. Maybe she was finally cracking up. The weariness of working so hard for the last few months were getting to her as well as the past terrifying twenty-four hours.

If Ace hadn't clasped her chin between his finger and thumb and started kissing her, she wasn't sure she would have been able to stop. She moaned when his tongue licked into her mouth, dancing and dueling with and around hers. When he pushed beneath the hem of her shirt, she whimpered and then groaned as his large hand caressed over her belly, up her ribs, and toward her breasts. She arched her breasts toward him and cried out when he cupped a breast in his hand, mapping the globe with his palm before stroking his thumb over the hard, aching tip. All exhaustion fled to be replaced by a burning, intense need that caused her womb to clench, her pussy to dampen, and her distended nipples to throb.

Ace released her lips before nibbling over her jaw to her neck. He laved a sensitive spot just under her ear and when she shivered, he sucked the skin into her mouth. She gasped and panted, canting her head to give him better access to that sensuous spot, and shuddered when he scraped his teeth over her flesh. He lifted his gaze to lock with hers and as they stared into one another's eyes, he slowly pushed her shirt up, exposing her skin. Goosebumps raced over her flesh as the cooler air breezed over her skin.

"You're so beautiful, darlin'. I can't wait to have a taste of you." He suited actions to words and tugged the cups of her bra down until both her breasts were exposed to his gaze. "So damn sexy," he said just before he lowered his head toward her chest.

Her lips parted as she sucked air into her burning lungs, and she closed her eyes as he swirled the tip of his tongue around the first areola before moving to the other. It was exquisite torture, and though she loved what he was doing to her, it wasn't enough. Delta needed to feel his mouth licking, sucking at her nipples.

She threaded her fingers into his hair and tugged him closer. She felt his chest rumble against her side and suspected he'd just laughed, but she couldn't be sure since she couldn't see his face.

She felt the truck swerve just as Ace sucked a nipple deep into his mouth and hoped fleetingly they weren't about to have an accident, and then she was once more lost in pure bliss. Ace alternated between flicking his tongue back and forth over the tip of her breast and then suckling on her nipple. She shook when he pressed her nub up against the roof of his mouth, crushing it to incite a small bite of pain. Her nerve endings zinged with electrical sparks straight down to her clit and pussy as her brain receptors warred with each other.

Delta had had no idea until then that having a little pain would enhance the pleasure, but that's exactly what it had done. Cream wept from her pussy onto her panties and her clit beat in rhythm with her heart.

Ace shifted his head to her other breast and just as he started suckling on that nipple, he tugged at the button on her pants and lowered the zipper. She moaned when his fingers delved under her panties, caressing over her mound and between her folds.

She widened her legs to give him better access, mentally begging him to continue, to make her come, but he released her nipple and withdrew his hand from between her legs. When she opened her eyes to ask him why he'd stopped, she became aware the truck was no longer moving. After glancing about she realized they were already back at the ranch. She tried to calm her rapid breaths, to regulate her breathing, but when she met first Major's heated gaze and then Rocco's, she shook with need.

And then all the men seemed to move at once.

Ace pulled the zipper of her pants up, opened the door, and tugged her across the seat into his arms. He nudged the door with his hip, closing it, and then raced toward the house and inside. He stopped in the living room and turned to face Major and Rocco.

Rocco held up bags of food and said, "Food first. She skipped lunch and her belly's been growling for hours."

Her cheeks heated. She'd had no idea he could hear her belly grumbling, but then how could she have known?

If she hadn't been so hungry for food, after inhaling the delectable scents wafting from the take-out bag, she would have foregone eating, but it had been a long time since she'd eaten. In fact, she'd only had coffee that morning and she hadn't eaten anything since the night before. No wonder she was so darn hungry.

Ace reluctantly lowered her to the floor and held her waist until she was steady on her feet. He clutched her hand and led her to the sofa, seated her, and then sat beside her.

Rocco knelt next to the coffee table and pulled containers from the bag before turning toward her and asking, "Do you like Chinese food?"

She nodded and licked her lips. When Major sat on her other side he handed her a glass of wine and then handed out the beers. Rocco gave her an open container and a plastic fork. Delta was too hungry to wait for them and immediately dug into the food. She moaned as flavors exploded on her taste buds. It was a combination of sweet and sour, with lots of vegetables and chicken. She practically inhaled half the container before coming up for air.

When she reached toward the coffee table and the glass of wine, she noticed that Major, Rocco, and Ace were all staring at her.

"When was the last time you ate? I know damn well you didn't eat breakfast." Major scowled at her.

She took a sip of wine, put the glass back on the table and wiped her mouth with a napkin. "Yesterday afternoon."

"You didn't have any fucking dinner?" Ace signed his question quickly and although he mucked up the last word, she wasn't game enough to point it out. He looked so angry she was worried he might explode.

"I ate around four yesterday afternoon. I didn't have dinner because I wasn't hungry."

"That stops now." Ace pointed his finger at her. "From now on you are to eat three times a day."

"I'm fine, Ace. I don't always have time to eat."

Major grasped her braid, tugging her gaze over to his. "You make time. No more skipping meals, baby. You're exhausted and I know the last day or so has been hell on you, but if you don't start looking after yourself, you're going to get sick."

Although it irked her to be told what to do, she knew that they were only getting on her case because they cared. And she knew they were right. She could also admit she been burning the candles at both ends and not taking good care of herself. "Okay. You're right. I'll start eating properly. I'll eat three regular meals from now on."

Major leaned down and kissed her cheek before pointing at her dinner. "Eat the rest, baby. We have plans for you tonight."

She sucked in a shaky breath and tried to curb her reawakening lust as she started to eat again. She glanced at her men to see they were eating just as quickly as she'd been earlier, and shifted on the seat when her pussy throbbed.

Rocco was sitting on the floor near her feet and while he consumed his dinner he didn't take his heated gaze off of her. She could tell he was just as horny as she was when he kept shifting from side to side as if uncomfortable. She couldn't stop herself from looking down at his crotch. She'd just taken a sip of her wine and when she saw the long, thick ridge in his jeans, she swallowed wrong and ended up choking. She coughed and spluttered as she tried to regain her breath, highly aware of Ace and Major caressing up her arm and patting her on the back.

"Are you all right, honey?" Rocco asked.

She nodded, coughed once more and wiped the tears from her face with the back of her hand.

Rocco reached out, took the wine glass from her and rose to his feet with a casual grace she hadn't expected of such a big man. When he pushed the coffee table aside she wondered what he was up to, but quickly figured it out when Ace and Major began to clear the food and drinking vessels away to the kitchen. Rocco grabbed a throw rug from the back of the sofa, grabbed some cushions and tossed them onto the floor.

"Come here, honey," he said as he held his hand out toward her.

She inhaled as she placed her hand in his. This was it. This was the night they were all going to make love to her together.

Delta just hoped she could handle making love with more than one man at the same time.

Chapter Seventeen

Leo sat in the lone chair in his temporary bedroom. He'd been lucky enough to rent a house with another couple of guys working for the Woodall brothers. He sipped on his beer and tried to figure out how to get the deaf cunt away from the guys she was fucking.

He'd been literally handed the keys to the diner and her upstairs apartment, and since there had been a couple of spares, he had access to the place whenever he wanted. The only problem would be bypassing the security system. He'd heard the security guy telling the men the bitch was screwing, that they would be more diligent in monitoring and protecting the slut. Luckily for him, he'd been working at replacing the door to her inner sanctum. He'd had to work hard at not laughing up a storm since he'd been the one to do all the damage. It was kind of ironic that he was being paid to fix the destruction. It didn't matter that the men of the small Podunk town were more vigilant and protective of women and kids. They were still too dumb to figure out that he was right under their noses.

As far as he could figure, the only way he was going to get his hands on that bitch was during working hours when the alarm was off, and that was going to be difficult. That big dude hadn't left her side all day long. How the hell was he going to get her if the men fucking her didn't let her out of their sight?

There had to be a way. He just hadn't worked it out yet, but he would.

That deaf cunt was going to die for having his brother killed and he wasn't giving up until he had his revenge. Once he got a hold of her he would tie her up and fuck her, and then he was going to slit the cunt's throat.

* * * *

Ace stripped off his clothes while Rocco helped Delta to her feet. He glanced at Major when his brother entered the living room. His brother had disappeared toward the bedrooms and he was glad to see he'd come back with all the necessary items they'd need to make love to their woman together. Major had brought a towel and a damp wash cloth as well as the tube of lube and some condoms.

Rocco was kissing Delta like there was no tomorrow and right now, there wasn't. There was only the here and now. He and his brothers were going to have to make sure their woman was so hot she was begging them to make love to her, but first they had to prepare her to take one of them in her ass.

Ace moved up behind her, brushed her long braid over her shoulder and began to kiss and lick the side of her neck. She moaned and when he pressed his cock against her back, she pressed her ass into his aching dick. He groaned as he reached around to her front and began to undo the buttons on her sleeveless shirt. Once he had the shirt open he caressed the shirt down her arms and off.

Rocco broke the kiss, staring into her eyes as he unfastened her shorts. When she reached out to grab hold of Rocco's wrists, Ace stopped breathing. He was worried that they were overwhelming her and had decided she didn't want this, them, at the same time.

Major, who was also naked, moved to her side and cupped her cheek in his hand. "Are you okay with this, baby?"

Delta licked her lips and nodded.

Ace didn't need to be a genius to see that she was nervous, but that wasn't a surprise considering she'd been a virgin. She was still so innocent, but thankfully she looked as eager for this as he and his brothers were.

Major kept his gaze locked with hers as he knelt and then tugged at the laces on her sneakers. When he had them undone, Rocco held her hips to keep her steady while Major removed her shoes and socks. Once they'd been pushed aside, Rocco shoved her shorts down over her hips and then Major pulled them off, too.

Ace leaned over her shoulder and eyed her sexy body. She was so fucking perfect with curves in all the right places. He wanted to spend hour upon hour touching that soft, warm skin, hearing her cries of pleasure until she was screaming in ecstasy.

Rocco stepped back as he tugged his shirt up and over his head. Delta was breathing heavily and starting to tremble with desire, but Ace wanted her burning for him and his brothers. He glanced at Major and at his brother's nod, Ace unhooked her bra and slid the straps down his arms. At the same time, Major hooked his thumbs into the elastic of her boy short panties and tugged them down.

He wrapped an arm around her waist and pulled her back to lean against him while Major helped her step out of her underwear. Ace was so hungry for Delta, he wanted to turn her toward him and devour her, but that would be selfish. This wasn't about him or his brothers. This was about Delta, about her pleasure and making her fly.

Ace splayed his hand over her belly, his fingers moving over her warm, soft skin. When she sighed and gave him more of his weight, he brought his free hand up and cupped a breast. She made a small whimpering sound, but he wanted more out of her. He wanted her gasping and groaning, arching and begging.

He kneaded the soft, full feminine globe and when her nipple hardened pressing into his hand, he bent his head and began sucking on her neck as he squeezed her hard bud between his finger and thumb.

Delta gasped.

When she shifted on her feet he glanced down to see that Major had urged her to widen her thighs and he was grasping her hips. Ace brought his other hand up to envelope her other breast so he could stimulate both of her nipples at once. Major leaned closer to her pussy and blew on her mound.

Delta groaned, her legs trembling even more, and when his brother licked at her pussy she cried out. He tightened his hold on her breasts when her legs buckled and as Major shoved to his feet, Ace swept her up into his arms. He carried her to the middle of the rug and pillows on the floor and lowered her onto her back.

Rocco moved toward her feet, knelt and wrapped his arms around her thighs, hooking her legs over his shoulders.

Ace laid on one side of her and Major took the other.

It was time to prepare their woman to take all of them.

* * * *

Delta was shaking with need and she couldn't catch her breath no matter how fast she panted.

Her pussy was so wet, juices had coated the inside of her thighs, and her nipples were so hard, they were throbbing.

When Rocco knelt between her legs and then hooked her knees over his shoulders, she stopped breathing altogether. Her heart was racing inside of her chest and every time it beat, her clit seemed to pulse in sync.

Ace turned her gaze toward him and she barely had a chance to inhale before he was kissing her. She moaned as his tongue danced and dueled with hers and she kissed him back just as hungrily.

When Rocco licked over her clit she cried out and tilted her head back as she arched her hips up. Major chuckled, his warm breath caressing over her nipple and then he sucked the peak into his mouth.

She was so needy for her men, she was trembling so hard, she hoped her bones didn't rattle.

Major was caressing up and down her sides and belly as he suckled on first one breast and then the other. Ace was devouring her mouth with wild carnality that set her blood on fire.

Rocco was licking and lapping at her clit, driving her crazy as he rimmed her slick entrance with a finger.

And then he pushed inside.

Delta moaned as her nerve endings lit up, the pleasurable friction and overwhelming sensations driving her out of her mind. The pressure in her womb grew tauter and tauter, but not enough to send her over the peak. She shook when he added another finger and began to thrust them in and out while licking and sucking on her clit. Her pussy clenched, sending more cream weeping from her hole to drip down onto her inner thighs.

She groaned when Rocco stilled his pumping fingers and then tensed when he pressed his thumb against her pucker.

Ace nipped at her lips and then kissed his way down toward her breast. Major released the nipple he'd been suckling on and lifted his gaze to hers.

"Take a deep breath and relax, baby." He slanted his mouth over hers, kissing her voraciously, creating more fiery heat in her blood.

She cried out when Ace scraped the edge of his teeth over her nipple and then drew it into his mouth. His tongue swirled over the tip and then flicked back and forth sending sparks of pleasure shooting down to her pussy.

Rocco laved the flat of his tongue over her clit and began to breach her ass with his thumb. It felt so good, she bowed up trying to take him deeper. She couldn't believe how sensitive she was or how amazing it felt to have his thumb inside of her back entrance.

When Rocco began thrusting his thumb in an out of her ass while pumping his fingers in and out of her pussy, she knew she wasn't going to last. This time as she began to the climb toward the peak, there no slow build up. She went racing toward the stars.

She groaned with frustration when Rocco stopped again. Ace was still licking her nipple, but Major was no longer kissing her. When she saw Major move, she glanced his way in time to see him passing something to Rocco.

Rocco must have seen her watching because he lifted his hand to show her the tube of lube. Heat slithered through her body, centering in her womb and pussy, causing her walls to clench.

"Are you nervous, honey?" Rocco asked.

Delta shook her head, but then quickly changed to a nod. Major clasped her chin, turning her gaze to his. "We'll go slow, baby. If you don't like it, all you have to do is say stop. Okay?"

"Okay," she said, hoping she wasn't speaking too loud, but she was too caught up in what they had planned for her to be overly worried about it.

When Rocco pressed two cool moist fingers against her star, she shuddered because of the stark contrast. She was so hot, and the lube felt really cold against her heated skin.

Ace released her breast, grasped her wrist and then brought her hand to his chest. She caressed over his warm skin and bulging muscles, tracing the ridges of each defined muscle as she worked her way down toward his groin. When he shifted up on his knee, and canted his hips toward her, she didn't hesitate to give him what he wanted.

Delta wrapped her hand around his hot, hard cock and began to stroke up and down, watching his face intently so she'd know what he liked. When she got to the head of his dick, she gave a little squeeze and was pleased when he threw his head back.

Rocco caressed over her pucker and she moaned when he pressed two fingers into her ass. It felt weirdly amazing to have her anus breached, and while she felt too full and too stretched, she craved more. A groan got trapped in her throat when he began to pump his fingers in and out of her rosette. She sobbed with pleasure when he lowered his head and began to lap and suck on her clit again. Fiery need surged through her blood, her womb, pussy and ass.

Liquid desire pooled low in her belly and dripped from her pussy. Her internal muscles clenched and released and the coil began to gather in tighter and tighter. She quaked when Rocco added yet another finger, moaning and gasping through the burning, pinching pain of being stretched more than she expected. And yet she still craved more.

She bucked her hips up toward his mouth when he licked her folds from top to bottom, where he paused to dip his tongue into her creamy well, before taking the return journey. Her clit pulsed and engorged each time he swirled and then flicked it with his tongue, until she felt as if she was about to go out of her mind with desirous need.

His fingers moved in and out of her ass, the friction so intensely good, she wasn't sure if she could bear it. The coil was so tight she couldn't stay still, rolling her head back and forth on the cushion beneath. And then everything inside her froze. Delta hovered right on the precipice of something so tremendously big, she was a little scared to reach for it.

And then she was falling.

She screamed with rapture as she splintered into a million tiny fragments. Her whole body convulsed with orgasm and cream gushed from her pussy. The quaking and quivering in her muscles was so strong, she had no way to stop them.

Each time Rocco thrust his fingers into her ass and licked over her clit, another paroxysm shuddered through her frame. Major and Ace bit and sucked at her nipples until at last the spasms began to lessen and finally cease.

All three of her men caressed her skin, her arms, her belly, and her legs, easing her back into her body and down from such an ecstatic high.

She opened her eyes as she gasped in breath after breath and wondered if she'd survive all three of them making love to her.

* * * *

Major was so hungry for Delta he couldn't wait any more. His cock was so fucking hard he was aching, and pre-cum was leaking from the tip.

He wrapped an arm around her waist, rolled her onto her side and pulled her against his body. When he had her perfectly aligned with him, he rolled them both until he was on his back and she was draped over him. He grasped her hips and with Rocco's help, lifted her up onto her knees until she was straddling his hips.

He was about to reach down to hold his cock up so she could take him inside that sweet sexy body, but she beat him to it. A groan rumbled up in his chest when she pumped him a few times and when he felt the tip of his dick kiss her entrance, the breath stuttered in his lungs.

He forced his heavy lids up and locked gazes with her, hoping she could see how much she'd come to mean to him, even though he hadn't said the words. However, he was the one in awe when he saw love in her beautiful, jade green eyes. Tears actually stung the back of his eyes and he had to blink to keep them at bay. That had never happened to him before. He'd never felt so much love, so much completeness to another person so that he was nearly reduced to tears.

When she lowered herself down onto his cock, he had to grit his teeth so he didn't grab her hips harder and slam her down hard and fast. She was so fucking, hot, wet, and tight he needed to be buried so deeply inside of her that he touched her womb.

She worked her way up and down on his hard shaft, lifting and lowering on his cock in a slow, hot, liquid slide that was driving him insane. He ground his jaw down hard when he felt her walls rippling around and gripping his dick, which had his muscles tensing even more.

He didn't even realize he was digging his fingers into the skin at her hips until she clasped hold of his forearms for added leverage.

The sound of her sexy voice washed over him making him shiver and his balls to crawl up closer to his body. "Help me. Move, Major."

He nodded in acknowledgment, lifted her up slightly and then slammed her down hard and fast. She cried out and he paused, scared he'd hurt her by driving in so fast and deep. That was until she spoke once more. "Again."

He shook his head, and then glanced at Rocco and nodded.

* * * *

Rocco had prepared while Delta was taking Major's dick into her pussy. He'd slathered his hard, condom-covered cock with copious amounts of lube so that when he penetrated her ass she wouldn't feel any pain. He drew in a deep breath trying to quell the hunger raging through his blood and moved up behind her.

She shivered when he caressed down her back and then he gripped her ass cheeks, squeezing and kneading the sexy globes making her moan. Major moved his hands from her hips up to her ribs, intent on helping him hold her still while he worked his cock into her ass.

Rocco sucked in another breath, grabbed the base of his cock and aligned the tip with her ass. He pressed against her star and growled when the head penetrated her tight muscles. She was so fucking tight and she was clenching all around him as if she was trying to suck him in deeper.

He hadn't noticed he'd closed his eyes until he felt the air move against his skin. When he opened them again, it was to see Ace was kissing her passionately and Major was rubbing over her clit.

Rocco eased in another inch when her muscles loosened and then drew back to press in again. All the while he worked his cock into the depths of her hot, tight ass, he prayed he'd be able to hold off coming until Delta did. There was no way in hell he was going off before she'd found her pleasure first.

By the time he was deep in her ass with his pubis against her butt cheeks, he was sweating up a storm and shaking with need. He nudged Ace's shoulder, silently telling his brother he needed to hurry the hell up.

* * * *

Ace broke the kiss and shifted higher onto his knees so that all Delta had to do was lean to the side and take his hard cock into her mouth. She was trembling and moaning and she was the sexiest, most gorgeous woman he'd ever seen. Her lips were red and kiss-swollen, her skin was flushed with desire, and her eyes were glazed over with passion.

She blinked as if to bring him into focus and then her gaze dropped to his hard cock. He groaned when she licked her lips and he gasped when she wrapped her hand around his dick and began to pump her hand up and down. Although he would have loved her doing that until he'd climaxed, right now he needed to feel her mouth on his cock.

He nudged her chin up so that her gaze met his again. "Take me in your mouth, darlin'."

She nodded, licked her lips yet again, and then lowered her head toward his dick.

Ace didn't notice that he was holding his breath until the air exploded from his lungs when she licked over the tip of his dick. He groaned when she swirled her tongue around the head and gasped when she sucked him deeper into her mouth.

She started off slow, as if she was trying to find her rhythm, and each time she took him back into her mouth her confidence seemed to grow. When she started pumping her hand while sucking on his cock, he wasn't sure he was going to last. Her mouth was so fucking hot and each time she took him back into her depths, she sucked in her cheeks, adding to his pleasure.

* * * *

Delta was on fire. She couldn't believe she'd had no trouble taking Rocco's cock in her ass, and now that she had Ace's cock in her mouth, as well as Major's dick in her pussy, she felt complete. She was so full and yet it all felt so right. Tears burned her eyes as her heart and soul filled with love and happiness.

She hadn't even realized that pieces of her were missing until Major, Rocco, and Ace came into her life and she intended to hang onto them tightly, with no intentions of ever letting go.

As she drew up over Ace's cock, Rocco retreated from her ass. When she slid her mouth back over Ace's dick, taking him as far as she could, Rocco stroked back into her ass and Major drew from her pussy.

Her heart beat faster, pushing the blood into her pussy and clit, breasts and nipples until they were full and throbbing. Every inch of her skin was hypersensitive. Every brush of skin, touch, kiss and stroke on and into her body sent sparks of rapturous electricity shooting all over her frame, which seemed to center into her womb, pussy, clit and ass.

She moved faster over Ace's cock, bobbing her head up and down while stroking what she couldn't fit into her mouth with her hand. Even though she couldn't hear, she could feel vibrations rumbling from their bodies to hers each time they gasped and groaned.

The fire racing through her veins began to flame hotter and brighter as the wet, gliding friction set her nerve endings alight. Tension invaded her muscles bringing her internal walls closer together. Major was pinching and plucking at her nipples and Rocco was caressing a hand anywhere he could reach while his other hand kneaded and squeezed a butt cheek.

Streaks of bright light began to flash in front of her eyes and she moaned when Ace's sweet salty essence spilled onto her tongue. Her pussy rippled around Major's pistoning cock as her ass clenched around Rocco's dick as he stroked in and out.

And then she was right there on the edge of the cliff, staring into the dark carnal abyss of ecstasy.

Ace threaded his fingers into her braided hair at the back of her neck and began to rock his hips, sliding his cock in and out of her mouth. She reached over, cupped his sac, and rolled his balls gently in the palm of her hand.

She cut off her screams of nirvana as she toppled over the edge into her climax when Ace started to come in her mouth. She gulped and groaned as she drank down his delicious tasting cum. Shivers shuddered through her whole body as she imploded. Her internal muscles clamped and released, clenched and let go, over and over.

Ace withdrew his cock from her mouth as the last pulse faded. She cried out as Rocco and Major drove into her ass and pussy hard, deep and fast. They slammed into her depths at the same time. Another orgasm washed over her before the first one waned and this time she flew straight up toward the stars.

She quaked and quivered, gasping for air as cream flowed from her pussy. Rocco pumped into her twice more and then ground his hips into her as he came, feeling his hot semen spewing deep into her back entrance even though he was wearing a condom.

Major gripped her ribs firmly and shoved in deep. His cock twitched and pulsed as he orgasmed, filling her pussy and womb with his juices.

Delta slumped down onto Major, aftershocks still wracking her body as she tried to get her breath back. Even though she was replete with satiation, she also felt invigorated. Love, happiness, and adrenaline surged through her blood until she felt as if she was floating on a cloud of euphoria. However, she knew it wouldn't be long before she was fighting off sleep as the adrenaline dissipated from her system.

She braced her hands on Major's chest and pushed herself upright until she was sitting on his thighs.

Rocco kissed her neck and shoulder before he eased his softening cock from her ass. Ace was lying on his back on the floor with his arm over his eyes. She tapped his leg to get his attention and then curled her finger at Rocco.

Ace sat up and moved aside so Rocco could sit beside him. Major was watching her intently as he caressed his hands up and down her sides, leaving goosebumps in his wake.

"I love you," she said and signed as she met each of their gazes. "I love you all, very much."

Major sat up and wrapped his arms around her waist hugging her tight. And while it was awkward, Ace and Rocco each grasped hold of one of her hands.

"I love you, darlin'." Ace kissed the back of her hand.

"I love you, honey." Rocco squeezed her hand and the leaned in to kiss her.

"I love you, Delta Sykes." Major kissed her passionately.

When he released her mouth, he glanced over at his brothers and nodded. Rocco and Ace, with Major's help, lifted her to her feet. Major stood and then walked to stand in between his brothers.

They all went down on one knee at the same time.

She stared at them with tears in her eyes and didn't care that she was sticky with sweat or that she had their combined juices dripping from her body. There was so much love in their eyes, she couldn't stop her own eyes from welling with tears. She wiped the moisture away and gasped when they all signed and spoke at the same time.

"Will you marry us, Delta?"

There was only one answer she could give. "Yes!"

Chapter Eighteen

Leo waited until the diner was full of people to make his move. The diner had reopened just over a week ago and though he'd been itching to get his hands on that bitch, he'd made himself wait. His patience was going to pay off.

While the men she was screwing had been alternating staying with her while she worked, he hoped they'd become complacent and less vigilant since everything had been quiet. He been sitting in his truck for just over two hours watching and waiting. When he saw that old man and his crony friend get out of their brand-new truck, he knew what he was going to do.

He waited until the elderly men ambled into the diner and took their seats, and after making sure no one was around or watching him from any of the other shop windows, he got out of his truck and weaved his way through the parked cars. After another cursory glance around he got down onto his hands and knees and rolled beneath the shiny black vehicle.

Luckily for him, he had his own set of tools and always carried them with him in the back of his own truck. He rolled under the belly of the vehicle, pulled his electric screwdriver from his pocket and started drilling into the gas tank until there was a small hole.

Now all he had to do was get out from under the truck and flick a lighted match at the quickly spreading gas. He was going to have to run fast before the truck blew. He needed to get to the back of the diner and be ready to enter so he could get to that cunt.

Hopefully, the noise of the explosion would bring people running from every direction and he'd have his vengeance.

Leo rolled out from under the truck and crouched on the balls of his feet, once again making sure no one was watching him. He drew in a deep breath as he pulled the matches from his pocket and tensed his muscles in readiness.

He scraped the match on the box and flicked it into the gas and took off fast. His heart raced in his chest and he gasped air into his lungs as he ran. Once he was behind the building, he slowed down and breathed deeply to regulate his breathing as he pushed the spare key to the diner into the rear door keyhole and silently counted in his head.

When the blast came, it was so loud it hurt his eardrums and the ground shook beneath his feet. He turned the key and counted to twenty before opening the door. He knew as soon as he entered that the place was virtually empty since there was no chatter or the clinking of cutlery on plates. Leo just hoped that the guy on bodyguard duty had gone out the front like everyone else, but if he hadn't, he would deal with him, too.

Excitement raced through his bloodstream. He was so close to getting his revenge he could taste it.

* * * *

Ace's heart slammed against his ribs as the building shook when something exploded. He was immediately transported back to his last tour in Afghanistan. His hands clenched and he moved his arms as if he was holding his automatic rifle, spinning and scoping trying to find the enemy. When his gaze alighted on Delta he was brought back to the present.

Her face was pale, her eyes wide, and she was gasping for breath. He glanced over at Enya to see she was just as pale as his woman, and though he wanted to go and see what the fuck was happening, he didn't want to leave the women alone.

"Are you okay?" Ace asked meeting both their gazes.

"Yes," Enya answered.

"We're fine, Ace," Delta signed. "Was that an earthquake?"

"No, darlin'." He walked over to her and wrapped his arms around her, hugging her tight. She drew back to gaze at him.

"What was it?"

"Something exploded."

"What? Oh. What if someone's hurt? You need to go and see if you can help."

Ace shook his head. He didn't want to leave the women alone. "There are sure to be other men already out there helping."

"Has someone called the sheriffs and the paramedics?" Delta asked.

"I will." Enya raced to the phone just inside the doorway.

"Someone help."

Ace released Delta and started for the door, but stopped to glance back at her. He turned and signed quickly, glad that Major had given him and Rocco an intense crash course in sign language. He wasn't as good as his older brother, but he was getting there.

"Someone needs help, darlin'. Promise me you and Enya will stay here, in the kitchen."

"I promise. Go."

He nodded and hurried out to dining section. When he saw the elderly woman slumped in her seat, he cursed and hoped she wasn't having a heart attack. He raced over and crouched down feeling for her pulse.

* * * *

Leo entered the back door just in time to see the big guy who'd been guarding the bitch disappear toward the front of the diner. He smiled and quelled the urge to whistle just in case there were other people about. He moved along the hallway stealthily, keeping his steps light as he hugged the wall and stopped just outside the kitchen entrance. He listened intently hoping to ascertain if there was someone in the room with the deaf cunt.

When he heard a woman speak, he knew he had to make his move now.

"The sheriffs and EMTs are already on their way."

Leo sprang around the corner, his fist already raised and he punched the blonde woman in the jaw. She fell to the floor unconscious. Luck was on his side because the bitch had his back to her as she stirred something on the stove. He hurried up behind her, simultaneously wrapping an arm around her waist as he covered her mouth with his hand and began dragging her toward the door.

* * * *

Even though Delta wanted to go out and see if she could help, she remained where she was, in the kitchen just like she'd promised Ace. She sighed with relief when Enya told her the emergency services were on their way and turned back to stir the beef stew she was making for the lunch special.

Her heart flipped in her chest when a hard arm wrapped around her waist and large hand covered her mouth. She dropped the wooden spoon into the pot and began to struggle. She kicked back and clawed the arm around her waist with her short nails, but she missed his leg and he didn't even seem to feel her nails scoring his flesh. Delta sobbed as she wished she had longer nails, but she'd kept them short since she was dealing with food all the time.

She flailed her arms and thrashed her body hoping whoever was half carrying, half dragging her down the hallway toward the back would drop her, but it had no effect other than the tightening of his arm around her waist. He squeezed her so hard she felt as if her ribs were about to break, and all the air was expelled from her lungs. She tried biting his hand, but he had it cupped and she couldn't get his flesh between her teeth. After inhaling, she yelled as loudly as she could but had no way of knowing if her scream had been loud enough.

Tears welled and rolled down her cheeks. She'd caught a glimpse of Enya lying on the floor and she prayed that the other woman was still alive. Anger surged through her body along with terror, and while she was sweating she felt cold to her core. She was trembling and knew if she didn't escape soon, she was doomed.

Delta raked her nails, the tip of her fingers along the wall and her brain suddenly kicked into gear. Whoever had her was going to be taking her out the back door. She still had her arms free and planned to grab and hold onto the door frame for all she was worth. Maybe that would be enough to slow the asshole down. She kicked out again hoping to connect with the wall but the bastard was being cagey and keeping her away from the walls. All the while she was mentally cursing that the hall was more than wide enough so that there was room enough for people to pass each other if they crossed paths.

She was panting and her while her lungs were burning, she didn't feel as if she was about to pass out. Delta needed to try and keep the fear from taking over so that if the chance for escape arose, she'd be able to get free.

He stopped just short of the back exit and the arm around her waist loosened. She sucked in a deep breath and tensed her muscles in readiness. She'd never understand or work out how he did it while still holding her against him, but the next moment she felt something stab into her side. Lethargy invaded her muscles and her vision grew blurry. She tried to keep her knees from buckling but she knew she was going to lose this battle.

Delta slumped forward as whatever he'd injected her with knocked her out.

* * * *

Becca Van

"She's okay," Ace said as he rose. "It was the shock of the explosion, just a panic attack. Make sure you take her to the doctor for a checkup though."

"I will. Thank you, young man."

Ace shook the elderly man's hand, relieved that his wife hadn't had a heart attack like he'd first suspected. He moved away to give the couple some privacy as the guy tried to soothe his wife and gazed out the window. There was debris all over the road and on the footpaths from shop windows breaking, but he was pleased to see the firefighters were dousing the flames. While he'd been helping the elderly couple, he been attentive making sure no one came into the diner.

The sheriffs were also on the scene, studying the ground looking for clues. Ace pulled his cell phone from his pocket, sent off a quick text to his brothers and headed toward the kitchen. As he walked down the hallway a knot of dread formed in his gut and grew bigger with each step he took. He picked up speed and raced into the kitchen.

He took everything in with a glance. Enya was on the floor unconscious and Delta was gone. He ran toward the front yelling at the top of his lungs. "Get the sheriffs and EMTs in here now. We have a woman down in the kitchen."

When Ace saw the elderly man stand and hurry toward the entrance, he took off running toward the back, glancing into rooms as he passed open doorways, cursing his stupidity the whole time.

The exploding truck had been a fucking diversion and he'd fallen for it hook, line and sinker.

He burst out the back door, scanning up and down the narrow alley. He was just in time to see the back end of a dark green truck turning left onto the street behind the diner. Ace sprinted after the vehicle, hoping he was fast enough to get the number plate.

* * * *

As soon as he got Ace's text, Major's gut knotted. He and Rocco had sprinted for the truck and were racing toward town. He kept his foot on the gas pedal heedless of the speed limit, intent on getting to his woman.

He'd just hit the outskirts of town when his cell phone rang. Major hit the answer button on the steering wheel.

"He's got her," Rocco rasped.

"What the fuck do you mean he's got her?" Major roared.

"I left her in the kitchen with Enya to help an elderly lady having a panic attack. He got in through the back door."

"Motherfucking son of a bitch." Rocco punched the dashboard.

"How the fuck did he get in the back?" Major asked.

"I don't know. I have a license plate and a description of the truck." Ace rattled off the number plate, make, model and color of the vehicle. "Luke's running a check."

"Which way was he heading?" Rocco asked.

"North-east." Ace panted as if he was running.

Major turned the corner with a squeal of tires. "Where are you?"

"Just getting into my truck. I need to disconnect. I'm expecting Luke's call."

"Call back as soon as you've heard from him." Major disconnected the call and pressed his foot flat to the floor. His mouth was filled with the acrid taste of fear. He'd thought they'd be able to protect Delta, but they'd failed. He didn't blame Ace for what had happened, because he had no doubt that if he or Rocco had been shadowing their woman, they would have left her alone to help the woman, too. It was ingrained in them to serve and protect. There was no way they could have ignored a call for help. That thought made him think the bastard who'd kidnapped Delta had to have been watching them.

Was he familiar to them? Was he a local?

When he got his hands on the fucker he was going to tear him apart with his bare hands.

* * * *

Rocco unclipped his seatbelt and climbed into the back of the truck cab. He lifted the seat and pulled out the rifles they all carried locked away in their trucks. He and his brothers never went anywhere without a weapon even if they didn't carry them around town. They had rifles in the house, which they kept locked away most of the time, but they all always carried their pistols strapped around their hips while working on the land. Thank fuck they hadn't had to waste time by going back to the house to get their weapons. He checked both guns and the magazines to make sure there was plenty of ammunition, making sure the safeties were on and then climbed back to the front seat and put his seatbelt back on.

His heart was beating so fast it was almost painful and while he wanted to yell with fear and anger, he clenched his jaw instead. He lifted a hand to thread his fingers into his hair and wasn't surprised to see it was shaking. Every time they passed a side street he gazed down the roads hoping to spot the truck they were in pursuit of.

Rocco had no doubt if Luke, Damon, or his deputies were scouting, as well. He just hoped if they were that they found Delta before it was too late. There was no way he'd be able to survive if she didn't.

* * * *

Delta's mouth was so dry, her tongue stuck to the roof of her mouth. She was drifting in and out of consciousness, and though she tried to push the fogginess from her mind and the lethargy from her body, it didn't work.

She knew she was in danger but the drugs he'd injected into her made her too drowsy for the adrenaline which had been coursing through her veins to shake the effects off.

The drone of tires on the road was hypnotic, and while she tried to keep herself from drifting off, she sank into sleep again.

* * * *

Ace peeled out of the parking space and pressed his foot down hard on the accelerator. The back end of his truck fishtailed until the rubber caught the bitumen and he clutched the steering wheel so hard his knuckles ached. He felt so guilty his chest was tight and he was having trouble breathing. It had been his responsibility to keep Delta safe and he hadn't. He'd also left Enya lying unconscious on the kitchen floor. He hated himself right then, but he pushed his emotions aside and tapped into the cold, unfeeling soldier he used to be.

He was already outside the town limits but he hadn't seen another vehicle, not even his brother's truck.

When his cell phone rang, he pressed the answer button and nearly sagged with relief when Luke started speaking.

"The truck belongs to Leo Stafford, formerly known as Leo Pratt." Luke paused to suck in a deep breath. "Leo's brother was killed when trying to rob a bank in Chicago. Larry Pratt shot Delta during the hold-up."

"Fuck! Where are you?"

"We're searching. I have all my available men on this, Ace. I put out an APB on the vehicle and Pratt. We'll know as soon as he's spotted. I've got Trent and Tristan Woodall searching his house."

"Why?" Ace frowned.

"The bastard was working for Woodall construction."

"Are you fucking kidding? Why the hell wasn't a check done on this fucker? He's probably been watching Delta the whole time. Please don't tell me he was helping fix the diner up?"

"He was."

"Motherfucking bastard."

"I'll call if we find him. Don't do anything stupid."

Ace ended the call without bothering to reply. He would do whatever it took to save Delta. He'd killed while he was serving his country, and he had no compunction about killing again to protect the love of his life.

* * * *

"Talk," Major said when he answered Ace's call. As Ace told him what Luke had said, he clenched his jaw so hard he was in danger of breaking a tooth.

He wanted to curse up a blue streak but was scared if he opened his mouth he would fall apart.

"There!" Rocco shouted.

Major squinted into the sun and saw the back end of a truck in the distance. He pushed his foot down harder on the gas pedal.

"I've just spotted a dark green truck turning left from off the S8 road heading toward the T11!" Rocco yelled.

"I'm on the 141 just near the T11 turnoff," Ace replied.

"I'll call Luke."

"You don't have to," Major said in a growly voice. "He's coming up behind us." He was glad that he and his brothers had taken time out to explore the region after moving to Slick Rock because he knew there was nowhere for the asshole to go. In essence, he'd trapped himself because all the roads leading of the T11 were dead ends. Unless the fucker decided to use all terrain, he was trapped.

* * * *

Delta came awake when she was jostled about on the back seat of the truck. The fogginess in her mind was wearing off and although her limbs still felt heavy, she was able to move them.

She shifted on the seat, trying to keep her movements fluid so as to not alert her abductor, and lifted her head to gaze around. If she could inch her way across the seat, she might be able to jump out of the moving vehicle. It had slowed since they were now travelling on bumpy dirt road. Hopefully if she was able to escape, she wouldn't do too much damage to herself.

She inched her way closer to the door and tensed her weak muscles as much as she could as she grasped the door handle and tugged. Elated surprise surged into her heart when the door swung open and she dove out of the truck door, tucking her head close to her body, and rolled.

The breath was knocked from her lungs on impact with the ground, and she'd protected her head as much as she could until she came to a stop. She rolled onto her stomach and pushed up onto her hands and knees, her breath sawing in and out of her lungs once she was able to inhale again.

Her limbs were quaking but she wasn't about to let the weakness in her arms and legs stop her. She lurched to her feet, staggered and then began to run in the opposite direction of the truck.

When she looked over her shoulder and saw the wheels sliding on gravel as the brakes were applied hard, she tried to run faster. Her legs were uncooperative and she felt as if she was moving in slow motion, but there was no way in hell she was going to give up.

She chanced another glimpse over her shoulder and screamed when she saw the man aiming a gun in her direction. She flinched and sobbed when a shot was fired and dirt sprayed from the ground to the side of her, and she waited for agony to rip into her body, but the pain never came. She took off again and her mistake was looking back over her shoulder once more, since her equilibrium was already so screwed up. The tip of her sneaker hit a sizeable rock and she went down hard, her head knocking into the ground since her arms felt as if they had the consistency of cooked noodles and wouldn't hold her up. Again, she pushed her palms to the ground, but her body was quaking so hard, her teeth were clacking together.

Her heart seized in her chest as she looked back yet again. She didn't need to be told he'd just engaged another bullet in the chamber and she stopped breathing altogether.

Delta closed her eyes, tears trickled from under her closed lids and she envisaged Major's, Rocco's, and Ace's faces. *I love you,* she sent out into the ether hoping they wouldn't take her death too hard.

* * * *

Ace's military training kicked in and he slowed the truck so he wouldn't send up a plume of dust into the air. He followed the other truck's dust trail and when the cloud of dirt settled he knew the fucker had stopped. He turned off the ignition, got out and opened the back door. He lifted the seat and grabbed his high-powered sniper rifle out of the lockbox and had it assembled and armed in seconds.

A lump of fear formed in his throat when the report of a shot echoed in the air. The anger and fear coursing through his blood fueled his determination and he climbed up onto the roof of his truck. Once he was in position on his belly he put the scope to his eye and aimed.

The fucker was standing over Delta who was lying on the ground and his gun was aimed at her. He had no idea if his woman was alive, injured or dead. Ace exhaled, inhaled and held his breath as he squeezed the trigger. His aim was true. He hit that bastard right between the eyes.

The fucker was dead before he even hit the ground. Ace slid over the side of the truck and sprinted toward his woman. Fear made it hard to breathe, but his feet pounded the ground. He hadn't taken his gaze off of her, but she still hadn't moved.

He was on his knees at her side before he even realized it, and when he didn't see any blood on her, he reached for her, but hesitated. Tear tracks marred her dust covered cheeks and her eyes were closed but she was breathing. She was alive.

He carefully shoved his arms under her and lifted her against his chest. Her lids fluttered open and her glazed drugged eyes met his gaze before they closed again, but the smile on her lips told him everything he needed to know.

Ace had gotten to her in time.

Delta was safe.

Epilogue

It had been a week since Delta had been kidnapped and she was fully recovered. She'd ended up with some bruises and muscle stiffness after throwing herself from the truck, but she was back to normal.

Poor Enya had ended up with a bruised and swollen jaw but thankfully there had been no fractures or breaks in her jawbone. She had ended up in the hospital overnight so the medical staff could monitor her for the concussion she'd had. Thankfully, she was well on the road to recovery.

Major, Rocco, and Ace hadn't left her side for the entire time she'd been mending, and while she'd wanted to go back to work, they'd argued so fiercely she'd given in. She hadn't been able to miss the fear in her men's eyes each time she'd suggested she was fine to start working again, but they were going to have to come to terms with her going back to work sooner rather than later.

Lilac had stepped in and was keeping the doors to the diner open.

Delta still hadn't had a chance to ask Enya and Lilac about going into partnership with her, but she had a good feeling about the outcome.

She still woke up every night with nightmares, but the frequency of reliving her ordeal was lessening with each passing day. Maybe in a month or two the night terrors would totally dissipate.

When Major moved beside her, she opened her eyes to find him staring at her. She reached up and cupped his face. "Are you okay?" she asked verbally. She was using her voice more and more, and each time she did her men's gazes heated. Delta had no idea what she sounded like, but from her men's reaction each time she spoke, she didn't think she sounded awful.

"I'm fine, baby." Major covered her hand with his, wrapped his fingers around hers, and brought her hand to his mouth. He kissed her palm and then scooted down until they were lying on their sides face to face. "I love you, Delta."

"I love you, too, Major."

"How does getting married next month sound?" he asked.

"It sounds perfect."

He shook his head. "No, but you are."

He, Rocco, and Ace were always saying such nice, sweet things about her, letting her know that she was loved, cherished.

She turned to gaze over her shoulder when Ace kissed her neck. He was smiling but the desire in his gaze had her body responding in kind. "I love you, darlin'."

"I love you, too, Ace."

Delta rolled onto her back and glanced down to the foot of their bed, where Rocco was lying along the bottom of the mattress crossways. He was leaning up on his elbow watching her intently. "I love you, honey."

"I love you, too, Rocco."

Love and lust surged into her heart and through her blood, heating her body. She hadn't made love with her men since before the kidnapping incident, and she needed them so badly she started to tremble. She sat up letting the covers drop down to her waist revealing her naked breasts, and then she turned onto her hands and knees, kicking the quilt down further with her foot and she pounced at Ace.

He clasped her waist and steadied her as she straddled his hips and then she leaned down and kissed him. When she felt the mattress dip, she knew Major and Rocco were moving closer, but she was too intent on kissing Ace to glance at them.

She moaned when large, warm, callused hands began to caress, cup and stroke all over her naked body. Cream gathered in her folds, her nipples hardened and began to throb, and her clit engorged with blood.

She was so turned on she couldn't wait another second and reached down between her and Ace's bodies to grasp his hard cock. She lifted his erection away from his body, toward her entrance, and sank down onto his hard shaft.

Ace broke their passionate kiss, wrapped his arm around her waist and then scooted them both into the middle of the bed. He spread his legs wide giving one of his brother's access to her ass.

She groaned when cool moist fingers caressed over her pucker and leaned up to kiss Ace again.

Major moved closer to her side, clasped her wrist and brought her hand to his hard cock just as Rocco began to press into her back entrance. She pumped her hand up and down Major's cock while Rocco stroked into her star.

When she felt his pubis against her butt cheeks, she leaned toward Major and took his cock deep into her mouth, swirling her tongue around the head of his dick before she began to bob her head up and down his length.

Rocco withdrew almost all the way from her ass, and when he surged back in, Ace retreated from her pussy. Each time they thrust their hips they increased the pace and depths of their strokes until their bodies were slapping together.

The fiery ache in her womb and pussy increased each time they drove in and out of her ass and sheath, and she sucked Major's cock faster and deeper until she felt the tip of his dick touch the back of her throat.

Major fisted the hair at the back of her head, and at the same time Ace began to pinch and pluck at her nipples. The wet friction in her holes drove her higher and higher toward the peak. The coil grew tauter, her internal muscles grew closer together until she was hovering right on the edge of release.

The next stroke of their cocks sent her careening toward the stars.

She shook and shivered as rapture held her in its grip as she climaxed.

Major's cock thickened and pulsed in her mouth just before he started to orgasm. She gulped and sucked drinking down the delicious juices until he had nothing left to give. He pulled from her mouth, released her hair, and fell onto his back on the mattress.

Rocco surged into her ass once more and froze, his body quaking and quivering, his dick jerking as he came deep inside her back entrance.

Ace lifted her higher up onto her knees and thrust in and out of her pussy hard and fast. His eyes glazed over and his mouth gaped and she felt the vibrations of his yell of completion under the hands she had braced on his chest.

Delta slumped down onto Ace and shuddered with aftershocks. He wrapped his arms around her back and held her tight.

She couldn't stop smiling.

She never expected to find love with such amazing men in a small rural Colorado town, but she was so glad she did.

She had a thriving business and friends, and she'd found the loves of her life.

Delta had turned her back on society's expectations and prejudices.

She'd been liberated from those figurative shackles and was getting married in a month. Major, Rocco, and Ace had shown her she could have everything she'd ever dreamed of. She was going to live each day to its fullest. There was no way she was going to hide ever again. She was finally able to be herself.

Her men and the people of Slick Rock had turned out to be her liberation.

Her confidence was growing under her men's love and care, and she was even dreaming of having her men's children.

The Porter men had opened her mind, as well as heart and soul.

They'd stolen her heart right out of her chest, but she had stolen theirs right back.

THE END

WWW.BECCAVAN-EROTICROMANCE.COM

Siren Publishing, Inc.
www.SirenPublishing.com

Lightning Source UK Ltd.
Milton Keynes UK
UKHW02f1233190218
318107UK00006B/1122/P